D0255047

The Woman in the Willow

Christine Dente

Published by BiggerStoryBooks

Print ISBN: 978-1-7350832-0-9
Digital ISBN: 978-1-7350832-1-6

First Edition

For the old woman in the willow who enchanted my youth with visions of ageless beauty.

Table of Contents

Fall

Obsessed by a fairy tale, we spend our lives searching for a magic door and a lost kingdom of peace.

—Eugene O'Neill

1. The Renters

The front door slammed. Again. The slap of aluminum and glass came from the new neighbors. Catherine had been watching those people move into the house beside hers for two hours now. The door banged every time someone tromped inside lugging an over-filled trash bag or a bulging cardboard box. Slammed shut again when they trudged back out to grab a ratty piece of plywood furniture or some shabby kitchen appliance. Catherine flinched with every whack. Why not prop it open?

Her stiff canvas hat concealed the glances she'd been stealing since they'd arrived in the late afternoon heat. A three-piece family in a rusty green Chevy dragging the smallest U-Haul trailer she'd ever seen. One mother and two kids, but that door had crashed against its tired frame at least a dozen times, disrupting what should have been a tranquil Saturday in early autumn.

The FOR RENT sign had dawdled in the yard for a year. Today, these people rolled in as if they owned the place. Good thing this wasn't some cramped duplex arrangement. Plenty of space between the houses. Catherine bemoaned the curve of the road though, which exposed their front doors to one another. And the side yards between them couldn't keep a single clap of metal on wood from making her jump, as if her old body forgot what it had learned a minute ago—or remembered what it had learned years ago.

Catherine Hathaway had turned seventy this summer. This ending of seven decades rattled her in a new way.

She knelt on the lawn, bare hands in a flower bed, rooting out weeds. Every inch of grass under her knees and on her property grew green and thick. Right up to where the neighboring lawn began, brown and clumpy. The difference was impossible to miss.

The thud jarred her to attention again. Catherine sat back on her heels to assess the situation. She squinted. The mother was rather young and plump. The boy was lean and pale, with a sandy-blond mop, probably ten if her memory of fifth-graders served her.

The chubby woman had sidled down the concrete steps and stood wheezing and leaning against the car. "Patrick! Paah—trick! Come out here now!"

The boy flew out the door and scuttled to her side. "Mom, are you okay? Did you take your medicine and drink enough water?" He stood almost as tall as her and easily placed a hand on her shoulder.

The mother brushed it off. "I'm good. I just need to catch my breath. Grab that box of cups and glasses from the back seat. And be careful—don't break anything." She waddled down the driveway, shouting over her shoulder. "C'mon, we're almost done, so keep it moving."

Catherine frowned at the ground and wagged her head. Too tough of a mother for such a tender child. Feeling the weight of her scowl, she lifted her lips and eyebrows to simulate a smile. Not that anyone was looking.

She remembered her shock yesterday, catching sight of her reflection in the glare of her own glass door. She was leaving the house and startled herself with that grimace, a side of her she hadn't seen. Like looking out a window and finding a staring stranger, her unedited face confronted her.

Why did she care how she looked? She could frown or growl or glare all day if she wanted to. She didn't see many people anyway. What good did her reflection do? More like a two-way mirror. She was forgetting which side she was on.

The neck and knees were certainly acting their age today. Not that she was in bad shape for an older lady. She was doing her best to take care of herself. Maybe even Mother would have approved if she'd lived to see her daughter reach seventy.

"Nobody does their best, Catherine, nobody," Mother liked to say, refusing Catherine's excuses for not doing something perfectly and using the line as a preemptive excuse for her own failings. And anyway, Mother died long before Catherine grew old, gone before her daughter's thirtieth birthday.

Catherine dangled a dandelion by its root, satisfied that she'd gotten all of it. Seventy was better than dead.

Beneath the brim of her gardening hat, she scanned their front yard for the little girl. A tiny scruff of a thing, the girl had flitted around on the grass in a dingy princess costume, unaware of her snarled hair and shabby dress. She'd carried some small boxes and plastic toys from the trailer, singing or whining about something or other. Catherine had glimpsed the back of her half an hour ago as she disappeared into the house, her figure distorted by the storm door trembling in her wake. Hadn't come outside since then. Only the beleaguered boy showed his face. And that irritated mother scrabbling back and forth, in and out, slam bang slap.

Catherine scooped the weeds and tossed them into her bucket. Her hands shook. She seized the plastic rim, her heart fluttering with something like guilt or even panic. It tried to rise in her chest. She breathed in through her nose, out through her mouth.

The familiar voices invaded her brain.

Miss Catherine, don't you dare get all tangled up in other people's problems. You've got enough of your own.

Old Woman, you'd scare the daylights out of those people with your lumpy nose and veiny hands. Spare the neighbors a visit from a cranky old lady.

Shame that mother doesn't take care of herself or those kids.

That family's a mess. Better keep your distance.

The mother wriggled butt-first from the trailer, hugging a half-open cardboard box. She staggered a few steps, then leaned against the dirty side panel, her face shiny and sagging in the end-of-the-day glare.

She'd glanced at Catherine a few times since they'd arrived in their new driveway. But who knows if she had waved. Catherine only lowered her eyes and got back to minding her own business. Why wait around to see if that short-tempered young mother would attempt contact? People in this neighborhood soon learned that you didn't have to engage if you didn't want to.

The boy reappeared. "Mom, Peyton won't come out and help. She's lying on the kitchen floor whining about being hungry. She says she needs a snack."

He spoke in a monotone, no inflections. So as not to incite his mother, Catherine guessed. He was the only one of the three of them who didn't slam the door every time he moved in or out of the house.

The mother huffed, slid the heavy box down her thighs, and dropped it from knee-level to the cement. It split open, pots and pans tumbling out. The woman squeezed her sweaty temples with her palms and shrieked at the boy.

"You tell her I said get her butt out here or she won't get any dinner tonight, let alone a snack!" Her voice cracked, and her face turned red as a ripe tomato. Hands at her sides again, she shifted her eyes in Catherine's direction, then dropped them to the boy. "Never mind, I'll tell her myself," she said through clenched teeth.

That voice. Just like Mother's: compressed and pointed for piercing a child's ears.

The mother pounded up the steps and slammed inside. The boy remained a statue in the driveway, stuck in the middle of their mess. Then he suddenly came to life again and began unpacking the car's trunk. Catherine returned to her weeding, her hands trembling, her neck registering its unrelenting stiffness. She must get out of this heat.

She pressed her palms into the soil, straightened her knees, and heaved herself up from the earth. Catherine stood nearly six feet tall when her back finally click-clacked into place. She pictured an old wooden roller coaster linking itself to the ratchet chain. Was she fighting gravity or surrendering to it? Either way, she was going along for the ride.

A wave of dizziness swept up the back of her head and crashed behind her eyes. She spread her fingers, extended her arms, and widened her stance.

"Catherine Hathaway, you'd better find your balance before you fall like a dead tree in your own yard." The sound of her voice startled her. She hadn't spoken in hours. Biting her lip, she let "the ladies" have their say.

Miss Catherine, you're overheated. Get inside.

Old Woman, get a grip and stand your ground.

The ladies were intruders Catherine had identified years ago. Either worried or critical or somewhere between, the ladies' comments were difficult to dismiss. She tried to listen from a distance, their sentiments always idling in the background.

Looks like those people left a sinking ship.

Yeah, and rats have a way of invading other people's space.

She bent to lift her walking stick, and a puff of air escaped her lips. Planting the well-worn hickory branch beside her in the grass, she leaned hard into it, squeezing with both hands. She rested her chin on top and slid her eyes sideways to the neighbor's driveway. Did they see her swoon?

The girl never came back out. The mother bent over the broken box, cursing and refolding the top flaps as if she could put it back together. The boy dragged a cracked plastic chair out of the trailer.

Catherine turned back to her home. The home she owned. The beige brick rancher's spotless windows reflected her skinny frame. The changing light transfixed her. That, and the new unsteadiness. What was rattling her so much today?

Shouts bounced off the brick. "Patrick, hurry up. Put that chair on the patio and shut the trailer before you come inside." The mother wobbled up the front steps, barking more orders at the boy. He secured the trailer's door, gathered a few scattered items, and followed her into the house.

The porch light switched on. Robins began their twilight song. The temperature dropped an inch. Catherine's stomach twisted at the thought of summer's end. The confusion that came with change. Just when she was finding her footing, the world was shifting beneath her again.

She rotated on her sturdy oak pole to face the road. The sidewalk sloped hopefully past her mailbox. A hop, skip, and a jump to the right, it broke off where a cinder block foundation foundered in the clumpy soil. Her gaze swept across the road. A few bold stars and a sliver of moon hovered in the indigo.

She'd lived in this neighborhood these six years now and still wasn't used to its emaciated appearance: rows of empty lots and half-built houses. A small wasteland of a real estate venture gone bad. Her home was one of the few built before urban sprawl crawled to a halt on the outskirts of her Southern town. She called it her disenchanted development.

But this was what she wanted, wasn't it? A place apart from the rest of the world, an isolated spot where she could live, and maybe die, alone.

An owl's hollow call nudged Catherine from her thoughts. She peered at the other homes huddled in the twilight along her road. They kept their distance with their two-acre lots. The houses on her side faced away from the wild pasture and woodland rising up behind this far edge of the neighborhood. Some were empty; others rented to un-invested families or under-funded single mothers.

Like this new little tangle of a family. Catherine turned from the road and stared at the home to the right of hers. How would she contend with these people? Would they invade her space, disrupt her peace and isolation? The boy wouldn't be a nuisance, but the mother and that wisp of a girl—they could be a different story.

Catherine, squinting in the dusk, frowned at the house. A light came on in a side window, silhouetting a small child's frame. That skinny little girl.

Miss Catherine, you'd better get inside before that child comes out and gets under your skin.

Old Woman, your bark has gotten so rough, it'll keep the toughest of kids from getting anywhere near you.

Catherine examined the bony hands wrapped around her stick, the mud creased in her knuckles and crusted under her fingernails. For a moment, she was that gangly girl Catherine again, the one who loved climbing trees and playing in creeks. She chuckled and glanced back to the window where the child had appeared. The girl was gone.

The last light of day smoldered against Catherine's side window and spread its gold to the neighbor's pane. As she turned to go inside, she caught the windows winking good-night.

2. A Fence and A Stray

Weeks passed. Leaves slipped into coats of orange, red, and brown before journeying to the yellow ground. Catherine wavered in her driveway, bundled against the cold. The messy crowd of leaves on her front lawn demanded attention. But first, she needed to get a sense of her new fence, size it up from an outside perspective. See how it looked to the neighbors.

She moved to the road for a wider view. The fence company had done a good job. The solid pine planks stood eight feet tall on both sides of her squat rancher. Like a castle wall, it marched in parallel lines down her lengthy backyard, leaving quite an impression on the landscape.

Catherine wiped her nose on her coat sleeve, looked over one shoulder and then the other. She grinned at the urge to salute the planks lined up like soldiers. Their knotty eyes did not return her smile. This simple yet imposing enclosure said, *Keep out!* Its message was clear if not loud.

A door slammed. The aluminum clang vibrated the iron-cold air that sat between the houses. Catherine's eyes darted to the new neighbors' porch. No one there. She muttered something about renters bringing down the neighborhood, her breath condensing then dispersing in the air. These people had been here for more than a month and had done nothing to improve the outside of their house. The kids didn't even play in the yard. The only sign of the family was their noisy car coming and going at odd times of day. And that banging door. No telling what was going on over there.

The early light brightened her pale blue eyes. Catherine lurched toward the stone path beside her garage. Her fist tightened around the walking stick. Strange how quiet the neighborhood was this morning: no birds or even cars stirred the heavy air. Too early for humans to be outside. Anyway, the fence had been up for a week, and she hadn't seen a single person who could complain about it.

She paused to yank a tuft of grass from a crack in the driveway. The ladies filled the gap with their conversation.

Miss Catherine, you're retired now and deserve your privacy. Keep to yourself if you want to.

Old Woman, who cares what people think? Eight-foot fences make for great neighbors.

And then there was the gate.

Catherine stopped short to stare at where it stood beside the garage. An eight-foot gate, shoulder-to-shoulder with the fence, an entryway meant only for her. It boasted a black latch and hinges with an iron band spanning its center, reinforcing its grim and flinty message.

Catherine laughed out loud. She may as well add a moat and drawbridge to her rough fortress. She admired the gate. It meant business: freedom for her, freedom from them, the invaders of her space in the back.

A frigid breeze brushed her cheeks. The morning's task nagged at her. Catherine turned and shuffled into the open garage to collect her rake and leaf bags. As the sky yawned awake, she scraped the last stray leaves from her browning grass.

A giggle rippled through the hush. Catherine straightened and rested the wooden handle against her shoulder. Her knit cap low on her brow, she scanned for signs of life.

Nothing moved. Just a chickadee twittering from a low branch of her leafless maple. She waved hello to the bird, then tugged at the edges of her old wool gloves, tightening them on her knuckles. The pair had holes in most of the fingertips from years of hard use. They had been Mother's. She couldn't seem to give them up.

Cupping her chapped lips, she breathed to heat her nose and cheeks. This cold snap had taken her by surprise. An early frost trying to rush autumn out the door. In the dry air, her wiry silver hair had flung itself out and around her numbed cheeks. Random strands clung to the edges of her black wool cap and the shoulders of her brown corduroy coat.

A robin hopped along the lawn, scrutinizing her work for disrupted bugs and worms. Catherine inspected her efforts, too. She'd left a solid line of demarcation where her lawn bumped against the neighbor's thick layer of leaves. No surprise there. The owner had barely cared for it while the house sat empty all summer. These new people hadn't even touched it, let alone cleared it. Autumn's debris lay where it had fallen. The back patio's broken plastic chairs and rusted grill had gathered their share of rubbish, too. Thanks to the new fence, she wouldn't have to see that mess from her backyard now.

Catherine lowered her chin and rolled her head from side to side. Her neck refused to release its grip. Maybe the piles of leaves would magically bag themselves. She looked up again. The naked maple tree blurred and waggled like a finger, warning her to hold still. Steadying herself with the rake, she trusted it to hold her weight.

A tiny figure appeared at the far corner of the renters' house. That skinny little girl in a bright pink dress. She stood beside the faded bricks, giggling and waving at Catherine. Catherine blinked, half-lifted her hand, but the girl had ducked around the corner. She frowned and bent to scoop the first pile into a large plastic bag.

The wind picked up. A pink flutter summoned her to the closest corner of the house. There she was again, the bare-footed girl, probably four or five years old, looking like a lost puppy but grinning like a wild dog. She pointed at something behind Catherine.

Catherine swung to see that mangy orange cat crouching behind her, camouflaged in the grass. The stray was waiting to see if she'd shout or offer it a handout. It had slipped into her warm kitchen once when she wasn't looking. She waved the rake to scare it away.

Catherine turned back to the girl. Gone.

She let the rake fall and adjusted her hat. Then she hugged the bag of leaves to her chest to crush it shut. A cry drew her eyes to the new neighbors' driveway. There was that wild child again. One foot in the street, hooting with her head back, holding the open lip of her mailbox.

"Woo-woo-whee!" The girl ran down the sidewalk past Catherine's mailbox, fast as a fox. She wailed like a siren, her hair trailing, her eyes a sideways dare. Catherine couldn't help but stare. The girl whirled to a stop where the path ended, stood high on bare toes with arms above her head, and pirouetted. After pausing to grin at Catherine, she raced back along the concrete, chin to the sky, breath billowing like steam from a locomotive.

Catherine gasped, certain of what the girl would do next. The kid passed the invisible boundary between the yards, circled back on the grass, and dashed through the leaves into Catherine's freshly cleared patch.

"Hey!" she shouted.

The girl wheeled and vanished around the corner where she'd first appeared.

Bratty little thing—like a feral cat!

A little pathetic and underfed. Probably bite your hand if you tried to feed her.

That creature had better stay in its own yard where it belongs.

Where's that mother? She should be looking for her.

Catherine clapped her hands, numbed inside her gloves, then folded them close to her frozen lips, pressing away a smile.

She got back to work, forgetting her neck. The wind worked against her as she filled the rest of her bags and piled them at the curb. She repaired the breach in her boundary and glanced at the girl's house once more. The vacant windows stared.

This trespass blighted the day's sunny forecast. But at least she knew what she was dealing with. A whirlwind of a kid, alive and kicking.

Something black and flapping caught her eye. Catherine looked toward her gate. A bluish-black grackle had settled on its curving top, keeping one bright eye on her. They exchanged stares before it flew away, griping like a rusty-hinge.

Mother hated all blackbirds. Said they were like spies poking into other people's privacy. Catherine wondered if Mother would have approved of her new fence and gate.

Catherine, she'd have said, *don't ask the world for permission. Do what you want. When things don't go your way, you only have yourself to blame.*

Catherine pinched off her tattered gloves one fingertip at a time, pictured herself dropping them into the trash, shopping for a new pair. Things were going her way here in this place she'd created. At least in her haven behind the gate.

A cold gust of wind swept in from the road. It spread the renters' leaves back over Catherine's pristine lawn. Eyes to the ground, she sighed and stuffed her gloves into her pocket. She dragged the rake into the garage and closed the door before any strays could slip in without her notice.

3. The Ladies

Percy greeted Catherine when she stepped into the kitchen from the garage. She knelt on the mat by the door to accept the little terrier's licks to her face. He wiggled and whined as if she had been missing for years and was suddenly back in his life. Stroking his head, Catherine admired again his thick coat of chestnut browns and ashy blacks, highlighted with patches of toffee-blond.

"I didn't want to wake you from your doggy dreams, sweet Percy. That's why I left you inside." She touched the tip of his nose. "And you like to wander toward the road when I'm not watching."

The dog's paws rested on her knees, his ears lifted, head tilted to catch her tone. A smile cracked her lips. "Oh, all right. Let's get you a treat."

He galloped to the cabinet and performed his prancing-circus-horse dance. She laughed, gripping the counter and peeling off her boots. Percy turned a few circles while waiting for her to slide into her slippers and shuffle across the spotless hardwood floor. She fished his treat from the bag and smiled. He scarfed up every crumb.

"My turn now, you little cutie." Catherine dropped a slice of bread into the toaster and paused at the sink. Percy at her feet, she switched on the light above the stainless-steel basin and washed and warmed her hands. A cloud sat on her chest, a fog clogged her head. She looked past her opaque face in the window. Had the early cold numbed her brain? Or had that kid gotten to her?

The ladies seemed to be knocked off their game, too. They stayed quiet while she leaned her hips into the counter, surprised by the silence. Catherine shook her head and dried her hands. This heaviness felt old and far away. But it was close, too, like the way her heart was in her throat. Catherine pressed a hand to her lips. Her mind sifted through memories, searching for images to shape into meaning.

She saw herself as a young teacher, her life a Tilt-A-Whirl: up and down, spinning around—the days left her dizzy and disoriented. Tossed about in the conflict between ordering her life yet finding it impossible to control a single thing in her day, she'd always assumed she was just a little crazy.

Decades ago, Catherine's kindergarten classroom had overwhelmed her. Wrangling and caring for precious children every day made her mornings a torturous exercise of willpower.

You won't make it through a single hour of school today. Better call in sick.

You're just lazy. Get up and get moving.

But extra sleep would help you reset. You're muddled and not helping those kids at all.

Staying in bed is not an option. Do you want to turn into Mother?

After years of this wrestling and far into her days as a fifth-grade teacher, Catherine recognized the ladies. They were the problem. Their ongoing conversation included catastrophic predictions from which she needed protection, and shaming critiques measured against perfection. Getting to know these voices better, she'd learned that one of them was a bit nervous and the other just plain mean.

The nervous one said things like, *Miss Catherine, you may never have a husband and kids of your own. You could end up all alone.*

The mean one would answer, *Damn it, Woman, look in the mirror. You're no beauty, and you're better off alone—in charge of your own destiny.*

Or she'd hear, *Miss Catherine, why did you talk about that sad student with the other teachers? You got all choked-up and exposed yourself.*

Answered by, *Yeah, Stupid Woman, what does compassion get you? Honest and vulnerable are a quick trip to a stomachache.*

On and on, they'd argue and tell her how to live a safer, more correct, most perfect way. Catherine lived within the tumult like a caged animal, biting at the bars of her life yet cowering behind the unlocked door.

The toast popped. Catherine's shoulders jumped. She smiled. The reverie had lifted her clouds like the years had weakened the ladies' power. Life had added its losses, but somehow she learned to avoid feeling all the feelings all the time. And she began to breathe, disengage. Let the ladies have their say without getting involved in the upheaval they caused.

Catherine drew a steady stream of air in through her nose. She folded the dish towel and placed it on the counter. She exhaled from her mouth and moved to the toaster. Pressing with the knife, she forced the hard butter to soften and spread on the warm bread, wondering if maybe she was a little crazy. Did everyone have ladies of their own? Did hers move in because being alone had opened the door?

Catherine took her plate to the table, sat, and patted the top of her knees. Percy jumped to her lap. He strained his neck against her hug, lunging toward the food inches from his snout.

"You only love me because I feed you, silly mutt." She pressed her nose into the back of his neck, his musty scent reminding her of all the stray dogs and cats she'd tried to save as a kid. Mother would never let her keep or feed a single one. She blinked her eyes, but one stray tear rode a crease down her cheek.

Before she could wipe it away, Percy turned and licked it from her face, searching her eyes with his soft brown gaze. Catherine let out a choking laugh. She reached for her breakfast, took a soft buttery bite, and offered him the last crusty edge of her toast. He snapped it from her fingers, then jumped down to search for crumbs under the table. As she watched him snuffle and sniff, a stray child raced through her mind.

Catherine stood in one swift movement, the chair tottering in her wake. Thunder rumbled in the distance. Percy bolted to his storm shelter under her bed. She settled the empty plate in the sink, then hurried to find her walking stick.

4. The Haven

Catherine eased the back door shut. Despite the thunder, Percy would beg for a walk if he heard her leaving. She needed some space to think without worrying about him.

She paused on the back steps. The air was still, as if holding its breath. But the forecast said the weather would skirt them today. The light had shifted to a brighter gray, and the thunder had moved farther east.

Catherine's scalp prickled as she took in the haven she'd cultivated these past six years: a flourishing world tucked out of sight inside her stunted suburban neighborhood. Here was her real life for which she'd waited a lifetime.

With a thrill, she surveyed the sweeping lawn. It sloped down from the house to the small creek at the far edge of her property. Midway clustered three old oaks, an oasis in the sea of grass. Small trees and flower beds bordered the inside of the fence on her right. Along the left side hovered mature trees, creating a canopy for her lush ferns and mossy paths.

This beautiful view was the reason she had built a home in this neighborhood. Retired from teaching for eight years, she stayed the first two in her duplex. The rented half-house with the classroom close by had been her world for decades. After weighing her prospects, she moved far from the school to the outskirts of town. Found a new perspective.

On this frosty fall morning, her haven captivated and calmed her. Her pulse strengthened and slowed whenever she stepped outside, especially since she'd added the fence and gate. Bolstered by her new boundaries, she could taste her freedom. No more nosey neighbors and vagrant kids. No more interlopers ruining her privacy and fresh plantings. She finally had her beauty and solitude.

Catherine shifted her hips to find a comfortable stance. Why shouldn't she have her dream for once? Why should she share what others wouldn't appreciate? Couldn't understand?

She pushed off the steps with her stick and landed on her smooth stone patio. The teak table wore its winter cover, but the wooden benches, well, she'd let them weather the winter. She walked down the gentle slope, admiring the sitting places and stone paths spread throughout her paradise.

Nearing the creek, Catherine squinted at a blue heron launching from the bank. It flew low and disappeared where the new fence ended at the water. She was disappointed to lose sight of the bird's path along the stream. But peace of mind was a fair trade for losing her wider view.

Maybe you should have your eyes checked, Miss Catherine. The edges are getting fuzzy, close-up and far away.

If you lose your vision, Old Woman, at least you'll be able to feel your way around inside the fence.

You'd better take care of yourself so you can enjoy another autumn.

Winter is coming, and you can do nothing to stop it.

With the fall had come the fading of Catherine's garden. Thinning branches and disappearing blooms. The young trees and shrubs had drawn their lifeblood close, leaving their extremities to wither and fade. Her ferns were buttoning up their fronds, preparing for the cold that would take many of their members. Little foliage would remain to prove their continuing existence in winter. Those giant oaks and beeches along the creek were letting go more slowly, some clusters of leaves still green and reaching for the sun.

Catherine shivered, taking small, careful steps in her old leather boots. She missed the warm seasons. Days of planting bare feet on the mossy creek bank, evenings beneath the velvet sky. Every morning and late afternoon in summer found her propped on a cushion in her slanting Adirondack chair. She'd lean back and gaze up into the canopy of her crown jewel: the old weeping willow tree, a beauty who had thrived here long before she came to create her haven.

Catherine stopped to admire that lofty creature anchored at the edge of her property. She'd always wanted a willow tree to call her own, one she could admire from a distance, like a veiled bride at the altar. Or enjoy up close, like a cozy cabin in a storm. Her soul longed to absorb the strength of those slender green branches, their grace as they flowed, long and luxuriant like a woman's fingers and hair.

Catherine's eyes traced the draping branches where they touched the ground. They were losing color and thinning too. She'd soon be a spindly old thing with the rest of her wintry cousins, shorn of her beauty and naked in the cold.

Something gnawed at Catherine, grated along her spine. She turned to the squirrel perched on her fence, chiseling an acorn. Ah, yes. He reminded her to check the fence's integrity. The elements did their worst when no one was looking. The temperatures had been swinging like a pendulum. One more thing to care for and worry about. She rolled her eyes to the gray sky giving way to the weak sun. This was as warm as it would get today. Better finish the hike down the hill.

5. The Girl and the Willow

Catherine settled in her chair beneath the willow at the creek's edge, the spindly branches encircling her. She reached to press a palm to the trunk as if caressing a child's cheek. Then she leaned forward to admire the willow's long toes emerging in the shallow flow. She scanned up to the tallest branches. The tree was a sentinel of sorts, guarding Catherine's small patch of land and also watching over the woods and meadows beyond.

She zipped her coat to her throat and leaned back in the weathered wooden chair. Chin to the canopy, she closed her eyes and let her mind drift, untangle, like limbs dangling in water. The face of that neighbor girl bobbed to the surface of her consciousness. What was it about that kid?

The temperature shifted. Competing breezes volleyed for position. A cool draft slipped from the creek's surface, slid up the bank, and landed like a pillow on Catherine's lap. The whiff of musty basement lifted thick and pungent to her tongue. Her nostrils sent a message to her head, which stirred a memory in her heart. Catherine smiled, following the scent.

She is seven again, wading in the water behind the apartment complex where she spent the first years of her life. The girl Catherine walks the woods that skirt Middle Creek. She maps her days with paths that lead her deep into solitude and far from the emptiness of the rented rooms.

She opens up like a wildflower, skipping along the muddy embankment. She struts like a wild turkey, her lanky legs loosening the farther she gets from the stuffy one-bedroom. This well-worn pathway in the midst of a wild place embraces and shakes her all at once.

Middle Creek reeks of mud and decay. Churned earth distilling a fishy brew. An oxygen-infused pollution, hungry fungus composing life from death. She wades in, sinking an inch with each step. The water swallows her shins. She shuffles her feet to save her creek sneakers from the sucking silt.

She loves this place. Crayfish brush her ankles in their backward escape from each rock she lifts. A muskrat cruises past with a waterline stare before disappearing into a hole in the bank. An occasional turtle snout breaks the surface, then leaves a whirlpool in its diving wake. The girl moves into the deepest and slowest parts of the little river.

The murky water makes Catherine's scalp tingle. Her imagination conjures gigantic carp, prehistoric snapping turtles, and slimy creatures she'll never see. They pass her bare legs as she glides downstream, the water lapping at her ribs. No one knows where she is. She could be swept away at any moment, a thrilling and shocking thought.

The girl Catherine imagines Mother discovering her days later in a hospital, half-drowned; Mother frantic after days of searching for her—missing her; Mother crying with relief and holding her close.

The chair's weathered wooden arm cut into her skin. A crow's throaty call cut through the drama of her daydream. Catherine's eyes opened.

She searched the branches. The large blackbird was perched high, rattling and cackling in its strange and hollow language. A few of its comrades joined the conversation.

Missing her cushion, Catherine adjusted her long legs and bony hips. Her eyes landed at the creek's edge, where a few flat stones laid a path to the other side. Whenever she crossed that bridge, it led her to places she could still be surprised. Whether happening upon the broad antlers of a buck or the tail end of a bobcat, her heart, if not her feet, followed these wild creatures making their escape. And when the mysterious rustles of life in the canopy and the underbrush would send her whistling her way home in the dusky dark, her face and soul were bright.

Her wanderings throughout those unmanaged acres accentuated the contrast with her home. Clean surfaces, predictable patterns, familiar textures, limited tastes. But the willow was her touchstone, whether coming or going.

The crows kept up their chattering. Catherine surrendered again to the weight of her eyelids. Her head dropped back against the chair. "Just a short rest," she whispered inside a slow exhalation. The tree and wild woods projected in shadows. She tucked her mind into half-light. Her body released and unclenched when she wasn't looking.

The girl Catherine reappears, standing before a mirror and calling herself *Willow*, a name she'd taken when quite young. Mother had scoffed at the mention of it, and Father was gone long before she could talk.

Catherine's old mind rewinds, replaying the scene where she'd tried to share her special name with an elementary school friend.

"My father gave me a secret name before he left. Wanna know what it is?"

"I thought your dad died?"

"He did. But before he died, he said he loved me and wanted to give me something to remember him by. A name that means beautiful and graceful. A name only he could say."

"But I thought you were a baby when he died." The friend folds her arms. "And why would he give you a name no one else could call you?"

"Because it's between me and him. But I'll tell you if you wanna know." She leans in close.

Her friend pulls back. "Didn't he do drugs or something and die because of them?"

The girl Catherine fingers a tattered hem. "I don't know—yes. My mother told me he was . . . oh, never mind. I didn't know him really."

She stops mentioning the name to others, practicing the sound of it on her lips while alone at the mirror. "Catherine Willow Hathaway. Willow Hathaway. Willow."

In her imaginings after that, a pretend friend begs her to reveal her secret name. In the various endings to the story, Catherine either dangles it in suspense until the end of the school year or refuses to reveal it at all, going to her grave with her special name pressed to her chest as they close the coffin lid.

Her favorite ending: she presents the name to a group of friends gathered at a magical haven in the woods.

She, the lovely princess, stands beneath a branching willow tree with a sparkling tiara on her golden hair. As she speaks her secret name, the girls' eyes widen, contemplating the beauty, the specialness of having such a name. Strong, tall, beautiful, graceful. *Willow.*

For years, the girl Catherine keeps the name hidden like a treasure wrapped in silk, tucked inside a tiny box. By the age of twenty, she has quite forgotten it.

As a college student, Catherine finds herself in a world of swirling uncertainties and personal insecurities. Because daily decisions can lead to dire consequences, she admires others her age who seem to take life in stride. For her, routine social interactions become wrestling matches. The need to control her environment and limit her exposure leads to isolation and loneliness.

"Catherine, you want to study with us tonight?" Her roommate, Connie, is an outgoing girl with wavy blond hair.

"I don't know...what time...how long will we...?"

Connie is moving out the door. "Catherine, it's just a bunch of girls getting together. No big deal." She tries to soften her tone, but her expression is sharp.

"Sorry, I know. You always ask. And I never go." She can't explain the panic that seizes her when surrounded by chatting, confident women.

Young Catherine somehow misses the boat that shows people how to cruise through unpredictable seas, taking waves at just the right angle. Instead, her daily voyage is a series of blind-sided crashes that leaves her dazed and drained.

As a young teacher, she uses up all of her energy instructing children and interacting with parents and colleagues. She has little left for end-of-the-day introspection and reflection. She fights to find time to simply rest and get ready for the next day.

It is as if the girl Catherine and her secret special name sink to the bottom of a still pond where the mud and muck of the years settle like silt, covering up what is left of the child. *Willow* lies forgotten, buried beneath reality and responsibility, dreaming of the day she'll be called back to life.

The crow's deep-throated cackle dropped down on Catherine's head again, close enough to shatter her reflection. Catherine's body jerked to attention. Her eyes flashed open. The light beneath the tree had changed. Her limbs were stiff with cold. She lifted her head from the chair's hard back, feeling betrayed. She'd only intended to close her eyes for a moment.

Catherine hoisted her body to standing. She climbed the slope to her home and left her dream behind. She passed the beds of sleeping perennials. Her heart on pause, she hoped for the pulse of birdsong and bugs humming in coming summer months. But the warm days had fallen behind her. The girl Catherine had left her stream of consciousness. The hard, cold future loomed.

6. Tazzy

"Shut up, Patrick. I'm not a brat!"

"Yes, you are! Mom says come inside and get ready. Why do you hafta make her mad all the time?"

"I'm not! I don't! I just wanted Kitty Kat Krunchies!"

Catherine heard the skirmish while watching Percy pad around the frosted grass searching for a perfect spot to pee. The argument came from the new neighbors' place. The kids' voices arched across the lawns and over the fence, buoyed from below by the heavy morning air.

In her slippers and nightgown, she hurried to a crack between the boards. She hadn't seen the renters or that crazy stray child since the leaf-raking incident. In the last few weeks, she'd only heard their car making its strangled start. Or smelled their garbage languishing at the curb. Some days, a bright scarf or hat waved from the bushes beside their front walk. Never the mother's face threatening inevitable eye-contact at the mailboxes. Just her backside framed in the slamming glass.

Catherine smirked as she reached the gap in the fence. Perhaps the woman was inside all day smoking cigarettes and watching television, maybe collecting her mail under cover of darkness. What did she have to hide?

Catherine leaned her cheek into the rough boards.

"You don't know what Mom is going through." Distress choked the boy's voice. His back propped open the storm door. He pleaded with his little sister who stood nearly naked on the porch. "C'mon, Peyton, it's freezing out here. I'll get you something else for breakfast. Pleeeze! Before Mom sees you barefoot. She's got a lot to worry about today. Don't make her mad again!"

Catherine could tell the fellow was a fifth-grader. She had experience with ten-year-olds caught in the middle of being the parent when the parent wasn't doing their job. That bratty little sister was stressing her poor big brother out.

"I'm not Peyton, I'm Tazzy. Mom says I can be Tazzy. And I want Kitty Kat Krunchies—why can't I have Kitty Kat Krunchies?" Fresh tears spilled down her cheeks, and her limbs quivered with frustration and cold.

Catherine popped her head back, checked on Percy's whereabouts—there he was, licking his paws by the back door—and angled her ear to the hole. The brother begged in a soft tone, trying to bridge the gap between his mother and sister. The girl bawled.

Her brother tried to ride the waves of her wail. "Okay, Okay, Tazzy. Look, Mom's run out of her medicine, and she's not feeling well. She had a hard time getting out of bed. And she's starting her other job today. We can eat at school."

Catherine tucked her chin back, closed one eye, and leaned in with the other.

The poor kid wiped his sister's cheek, trying to calm her.

"Patrick, why'd we hafta leave Dad?" she said between sobs.

"Mom said we had to get out of there." He stared into the house and lowered his voice. "Dad was drinking too much whiskey and doing scary stuff."

Catherine pressed the side of her head into the boards to catch his words. She struggled to hear what the girl was saying.

"Is Mom going to slap me if she gets mad again and . . ."

Catherine willed her ears to catch the muffled words of the girl. Had she said, 'slap me again'?

Catherine exchanged her ear for an eye. Framed in the small opening, the girl stared past her brother through the doorway. His chin jerked over his shoulder. He lurched back. The mother appeared: a blur of flapping flannel and dripping hair. She lunged, grabbed the girl's arm, and yanked her into the house. The boy followed, letting the door slam behind him.

Inhaling a sharp breath through her nose, Catherine hustled herself and Percy back to the warmth of the kitchen.

The house was dark. She ignored the light switch. At her table in the gloom, Catherine waited for the world to wake. The dawn lifted itself up and over the trees outside her window and gave her time to adjust. Saved on the electric bill, too. The humming furnace and brewing French roast were all she needed to warm her bones and brighten her mood.

The gray shifted to pale yellow and blue. Her counters and floors winked back at the sun as it moved among the clouds. She pondered the plight of those children next door. What was happening in that little family? The mother was volatile; the son was anxious and sweet. The daughter was sassy but sad. And afraid.

A lump lay like a mossy stone in her stomach. Mother's instructions rang metallic in her head. *Mouth shut and eyes to the ground, Catherine. We mind our own business so nobody minds ours.*

Catherine brushed her hand along the smooth wooden tabletop, searching for vagrant crumbs and hidden spills. Her lips lifted at the image of that little imp of a girl—straight as an arrow, arms crossed and adamant, despite her suffering.

What did that little devil call herself? Did she say, Tazzy?

Such a demanding little creature. Sure knows who she is and what she wants.

Doesn't get what she needs, though, considering how that mother handles her.

Don't bother about those children or what the mother is up to. You're done with all that.

Catherine sipped the last of her tepid coffee. In the previous forty years, she had opened up and shut down more times than she could count. She had taught children so lonely and neglected, her heart had broken in a thousand ways. Her classroom had witnessed children dealing with illness, physical disabilities, and chronic anxiety. She wanted to fix the world for them. But the world resisted fixing; it damaged kids instead.

She picked at a sore spot on her thumb. Percy scratched at the door, his eyes trained on hers. She shook her head. Years ago, she'd allowed him to move in and out through his pet flap, chase a squirrel or sniff the breeze as he pleased. But the possibility of him wandering off, getting hit by a car—she couldn't stand the thought. Last fall, when the rain and mud wouldn't stop, she locked it. Sealed it soon after that. He couldn't forget, wouldn't let it go.

The dog pawed again at the wood, whining.

"Sorry, Percy Pup, but I can't worry about whether you're in or out, safe or sneaking off."

Catherine scudded her chair backwards along the floor, stood, and took three steps to the treat cabinet.

"Here you go, my little pooch." He dashed across the floor and slid into her ankles. After he gobbled his snack, she hugged his warm body to her chest until he wriggled out of her arms. Settling again on the chair, she slid her toes under his belly where he lay waiting for his next meal.

7. Miss Hathaway and Fern

Miss Catherine, that fence is brand new. In a few years it'll warp and crack, but not this early in its life.

Old Woman, trouble has a way of sneaking in and doing its damage in plain sight. Too far gone by the time you discover the harm done.

Catherine stood on her toes, stretching to the top of the fence. An early inspection to eliminate any effects of neglect on her part. Her fingertips just reached its upper edge, ran along the rough ledge. Solid, no splits.

Her heels dropped flat, and her palm pressed to the face of a plank. The new wood looked good. The builder had assured her that it would endure the Southern heat and humidity. He had stained and sealed it to make sure the coming rain and occasional freezes couldn't do any damage either.

Catherine turned and flowed among the ferns bordering her flagstone path. Beginning at the left of her patio, the smooth stones wove toward the fence between spreading yews and lentil roses, then curved with the Dixie wood ferns and Japanese silver leafs along a lengthy stretch that meandered down to meet the creek. Paused on a mossy stone, Catherine cinched the sash of her wrap and assessed her sad little shade garden. Bending to caress the browning frond of a ghost fern, she thought of a little girl she'd taught her first year on the job.

Fern was one of the students whom young Catherine had come to adore in that inner-city school where she'd had a classroom of kindergarteners for three years. That thin little five-year-old had stark black hair, and skin so translucent she appeared to be a pale shade of blue. Fern's shy and sweet smile made Catherine want to scoop her up and hand her all of the candy stashed in the top drawer of her desk.

"Miss Hathaway, I'm drawing a picture of you with your hair falling down to the ground," she whispered one day as Catherine leaned in to inspect the child's work.

"Why do you want my hair to be down, Fern? You know I always keep it pinned up and out of the way."

The girl closed her eyes and lifted her eyebrows. "Yes, but Rapunzel's prince can't visit her in the tower or save her from the witch until she lets her hair fall down, down, down to the ground. You need to be ready. That's why I'm growing my hair long." The girl touched Catherine's head as if caressing a kitten. Catherine squeezed the tiny hand resting on her temple, then straightened before the sting behind her eyes could become a spring of tears.

The child turned back to her paper and crayons. Miss Hathaway's hair appeared wild and golden on the page.

Fern often came to school with her hair uncombed, her clothes obviously second-hand. But nothing about her was fearful or self-conscious. No mistreatment or neglect showed, as far as Catherine could see, and she did look closely. As a teacher, she was obligated to report any suspicions of abuse. In all her years teaching, she never had to make that call.

Fern, though small and timid, seemed to be free and fanciful as a forest elf. She was as sunny as her yellow crayon birds perched in her purple trees. A perfect picture of childhood.

She ignited a tug of war in young Catherine's chest.

On the one side, Catherine wanted to be a warm and open teacher for Fern and her classmates. Let the children's parents carry the weight of worry about their years ahead; Miss Hathaway could love them for who they were in her classroom this year. She couldn't control what happened before or after school.

The other side tugged her to shut down, close up, and protect herself. Caring too much, getting too involved, worrying about situations in their lives she could only project. This was her battle of *How to Be*. It had exhausted Catherine.

She stooped to rake her fingers through the leafy mulch, mounding it at the base of the fern. Her spindly hand shook a little with the task. She remembered how, as Miss Hathaway, she sometimes took to her teaching post like a guard in the watch tower: doing just what the job required, hovering over her charges but keeping a good distance from the kids. No getting hurt on her watch.

But at other times, especially as the years added up with lessons learned, with the love she'd given and gotten in return, she'd eased off of her distant attitude. When she was well into her thirties and teaching the fifth grade, she tied up her life with her work, became the best teacher she could be. The students liked Miss Hathaway—in fact, some loved her—and they also respected and trusted her, learned much from her, and knew that she always had their backs.

Anyway, it's good you never married and brought children of your own into this terrible world. You did your best for the ones already here.

Actually, you would have been crazy to look for love from some man. They just don't stay around for very long.

Catherine dropped her knees to the moist ground. A family of noisy wrens trilled along the path, then traveled up and over the fence. Smiling, she lifted a weightless frond like the chin of a child. That skinny little Fern had thrived and grown up and out of her care. Had likely found a good life.

But Catherine could never be sure if she was doing the right thing for each child: teaching the best way, serving the uniqueness of each student, watching for signs of neglect or abuse. Who could keep up or even get a grip with such a struggle going on? Had she done enough? Like Mother said, *No one ever does their best, Catherine, no one.*

Catherine's *How to Be* tug of war had pushed and pulled her throughout all of her teaching days. Like two dogs on a walk, one dragged her backward while the other forced her forward. She couldn't settle on either side of the battle.

Until now.

Catherine shifted her weight to straighten her legs and solidify her stance. Her days of opening up were over, her resolve as solid as the gate in her fence.

8. Witchy Woman

Catherine caught the conversation from behind an oakleaf hydrangea, one of three such shrubs lining the path outside her gate. The neighbor kids had come out in the cold and sat chattering on their back patio. They passed a bag of potato chips back and forth. They didn't see her clipping the tall stalks near the edge of their yard.

"Patrick, I bet that old lady is a witch."

"What are you talking about? What old lady?"

The little girl licked her fingers before dipping them back into the bag. She crammed them in her mouth, then flung a greasy hand backwards toward the row of hydrangeas hiding Catherine.

"The giant one that lives over there with the big nose and black hat and that cute dog." Fragments of chips sprayed from her lips. She pointed to the far end of her own yard. "I've seen her walking around in the trees way down there across the creek. She has a broomstick and waves it in the air and talks to somebody, but there's no one there!" She grabbed another handful of chips and shoved them into her mouth.

Catherine froze, crouching and listening from between thick leaves. Puffs of frosty breath threatened to give her away.

The boy sighed, got up from his chair, and grabbed a corner of the bag. His sister snatched it back and it split, spraying the last of the chips across the concrete patio. He plopped his arms on his hips and looked toward Catherine's yard. "You shouldn't make up stories like that. You watch too many dumb cartoons."

"No, Patrick, she was casting a spell. And the trees were starting to move their arms and talk back to her!"

Catherine stifled a laugh.

The boy answered in a parental tone, "She was probably just waving at some bugs or dumb old crows. Look, some birds are down there now, flapping on the log that crosses the creek. And the trees were just blowing from the wind." He knelt to sweep the crumbs with his hands. "Please stop spying on her. She might see you. Mom doesn't want us going near the neighbors, Peyton."

The girl hopped off the chair. "Tazzy is my name—Mom said it can be. Call me Tazzy, or I'll spin up a tornado and make your room a mess so you have to clean it again and I'll eat your pillow for lunch!"

The boy brushed the crumbs into the bag then crumpled it in his hands. "Okay, but the Tasmanian Devil calls himself Taz, and he doesn't eat stuff that's not food."

"Uh huh, yes he does. He eats anything he wants, and I'm Tazzy 'cause Taz is a boy name, and I'm a girl!" She climbed on top of the warped gray picnic table and started to spin.

Catherine gasped.

The boy rushed to contain his sister just before she fell off the edge. "Okay, Tazzy, please come down from there. Mom said that if we came outside you'd have to obey me."

The girl jumped to the ground and pushed her brother's hands away.

Catherine's shoulders settled.

"C'mon, Tazzy." He frowned and headed for the steps, motioning for her to follow. Instead, she went the opposite direction, ran far down their yard to the edge of the creek—Catherine stuck her neck out past the fence to see—hooted and hovered on the edge of the water, arms to the sky, then she circled back to the house.

The girl sang loudly and skipped around her brother. "I'm going to visit the old witch and her cute little dog."

"Stay in the yard, Tazzy." He refused to move as she circled him.

She stopped, picked up a stick, and poked his back with it. "Okay, Patrick. You can go play your video game. I won't leave the yard." She stuck out her tongue.

The boy lunged at her, grabbed the stick, and threw it across the patio. He scooped up the crumpled chip bag, glared at the girl, and tramped inside.

From behind her cover, Catherine took a good look at their small, faded brick house. It was rather dilapidated, a sure sign of internal neglect. She wondered if they had enough furniture. Or food. Hopefully the heat was on. The kids' clothing was inadequate for the cold. She was sure this Tazzy girl didn't notice, even though her coat was thin and her shoes almost worn through.

Catherine felt a small admiration for the child dancing in the grass, her coat now thrown to the ground. Her flimsy pink nightgown puffed out like a parachute. The grass was stiff from cold, but the child spun as if it were spring. The wind twirled and twisted her long blond hair in its fingers, adding to its tangle. She stopped, dragged the back of her hand under her nose, then wiped it along the side of her nightgown.

The girl stared at the bush concealing Catherine. Catherine held her breath behind the branches. With a skip-hopping dance, the kid landed on the opposite side of the hydrangea.

"Hey, what're you doin'?" She poked her head through the leaves where Catherine hid.

Catherine's scalp prickled. She straightened, stepped back, raising her pruning shears. "I'm working in my garden." Her voice sounded a little strangled and far away. "What are you doing?"

The girl tromped a few steps sideways into the open space between the bushes. Catherine moved to block her before she could cross further.

The girl's chapped little face was serious. She lifted her chin to Catherine. "Well, I was dancing and thinking of pop tarts and princesses, but Patrick said there wasn't anything yummy in the kitchen for me to eat."

"Where's your mother?" Catherine frowned and folded the shears against her chest.

"Well, she got a new job, and they make her work on Saturdays, and she says maybe she'll buy me some Kitty Kat Krunchies if she gets enough money." The child squared her tiny shoulders and hips, mirroring Catherine's pose. "Are you a good witch or a bad witch?" Her eyebrows cinched and her lips pooched out.

Catherine mustered a glare, then sighed and leaned close to the girl.

"I am known as Witchy Woman in this neighborhood." She spoke in a slow whisper. "If children stay off of my lawn, I am a good witch. If they trespass on my grass, then they find out I am a different kind of witch." Catherine lifted her eyebrows and tilted her head, letting a slight smile curve along her lips.

The girl stared, her greasy mouth hanging open and eyes wide. When Catherine finished speaking, the child clamped her mouth shut, the corners tugging down and quivering. Her eyes filled with tears.

"I *told* Patrick that you were a witch, and he didn't believe me!" Her voice shook and her hands clamped into angry fists.

Anger at the brother or at her, Catherine wasn't sure, but the girl acted exactly like that mother of hers. Catherine backed up, but the child stepped closer.

They stared at each other for five silent seconds across the fifteen inches between them. A showdown Catherine was determined to win.

The girl unfurled a fist and pointed a finger at Catherine. "There's a spider on your face."

Catherine stumbled backward, brushing blindly at her cheek. The child had hurried into the gap and was laughing up at her. While Catherine examined the length of each arm, the girl angled her head toward the open gate.

"Where's your dog? Can I pet him? Do you have anything to eat?" She turned again to Catherine, her eyes now dry and her face relaxed. She had moved on to more important matters.

Catherine tucked her chin to scan her entire front side. No sign of a spider.

"No, Tazzy—I mean, no, little girl. I have nothing that you would want to eat."

The child's body stiffened, her face hard.

Catherine softened. "My dog is inside napping. Now go on, grab your coat and get inside your own house. Your brother will find you some food." She made a sweeping motion with her hands.

The girl wrinkled her nose at Catherine before running past her and feinting toward the gate. Before Catherine could say a word, she circled back, plunged between two hydrangeas, and sped past her coat on the ground. With a whooping cry, the child spun in circles in front of her back door, then slammed her way inside.

A filmy ache shrouded Catherine's head. She rubbed the back of her neck with one hand, clutching the shears in the other, and lurched back along the path to the half-open gate. Her jaw was tight. She slid through the small breach into the backyard, the latch stabbing her ribs. She fought back by kicking the gate's corner, bruising her toe inside her boot. She turned, seized the black iron handle, and yanked the stout gate toward her. Its edge hesitated where it met the fencepost. Despite the friction, in slow-motion suspense, the latch lifted, slid, then clanked into place.

9. Mother and Baby June

The rain had cleared the air. After walking the woods on this brisk morning, Catherine's chest felt cool as peppermint candy, her head unclouded as the sky. Only one bout of dizziness while she and Percy walked their usual two miles. Crossing the creek on that slippery dead tree had been a little tricky for the first time, the world spinning when she'd focused on the water instead of the solid old log.

Percy waited beside her at the back door, panting and pawing to go in. Catherine balanced on one leg to examine the other foot. Sticky mud from the rain-soaked path had embedded itself into every groove of her walking shoes. She'd have to waste a few gallons of water from the hose, the sprayer set to flush out all the dirt. Plus, the mud on Percy's paws. No matter. She'd do the dirty work over her patio. It could use a cleaning, too. Double work for the same amount of water. She clomped back down the steps toward the spigot, leaving a lumpy trail behind her.

The dirt and imperfections of every day had always been a thorn in her side. She couldn't help but notice dust on her tables, stray hairs on her freshly cleaned carpets. She'd wipe counters and tables ten times a day and straighten books and papers that others were happy to leave willy-nilly. Order gave her some sense of control in the hovering chaos.

And she noticed every inefficiency, every waste of resources. From the elementary school administrators to the checkout clerks at the grocery store, nobody did their job quite right. Nothing was as it should be. No one as good as they could be. Including herself.

She recalled having this mindset even as a child. She kept the bedroom clean, all the clothes put away, the bed always made. And she held onto odd items, driven by an unfocused anxiety about running out of resources. She even squirreled away candy, delaying gratification, just to have something to look forward to on a rainy day. She was an uptight, upright do-gooder, who often felt guilty for not living up to her own standards.

Once, she stole two cans of peaches from the grocery store.

Mother found them tucked in a dresser drawer. "Catherine, why are their cans of food behind your shirts?"

"I don't know." She really wasn't sure.

"Did someone give these to you?" Her mother had no reason to believe she would steal.

"Well, yes." She remembered her motivation. "My teacher said we should have extra food stored. In case of emergency."

"Baloney." Mother scoffed at any teachers who introduced ideas new to her.

Catherine shivered and began spraying away the mud she'd tracked onto the steps. Mother didn't mind an empty pantry, but it made Catherine nervous. She liked to be prepared.

Percy trotted away from the erratic water spray, and Catherine wondered where she'd learned such a perfectionistic and responsible mindset. Not from her dad since she'd never known him. Not from Mother, because she had been the opposite of organized, far from responsible. Perhaps Mother had taught her how not to be.

As a girl, Catherine had found many ways to escape her disordered childhood. Sometimes she would disappear into the huge forsythia bush behind the dumpster. Its brilliant yellow branches formed a hidden cave in spring. By summer, it was a green cavern, dense and dark.

Other times, the girl would spend hours wading in the creek or letting a storybook take her where real life could not reach. Many a fantasy novel had disoriented her for hours after she finished reading. Often though, she had just lived in her imagination. Worlds of enchanted forests or tropical jungles crawling with wild creatures soothed the stark hours spent with her drunk mother. Or alone.

Mother was sometimes gone for days at a time.

Catherine shut off the hose. Settled on her bench, she dug with a stick into the deep grooves of her shoe. The memory of that long weekend surfaced in

Catherine's head. The weekend Mother had left her alone with her baby sister. The panic and fear appeared as fresh as yesterday.

Mother left in the morning, saying, "I'm going out with some friends today. Don't forget to change Baby June's diaper and give her her bottles. I may be late tonight."

Late turned into two days. To nine-year-old Catherine, it felt like a month of waiting and wondering if Mother was ever coming back. She recalled carrying her wailing baby sister, a five-month-old infant, around their tiny apartment, arching her neck to see if a car was pulling into the parking lot. The hours spent changing the diapers, heating the bottles of formula, and rocking the baby left her body and mind exhausted.

Mother showed up in the early evening of the second day, her face and clothes sagging. She handed Catherine a bag of cold french fries and a burger, took the baby from her, and said, "Thanks, sweetie."

Before Baby June had come along, Mother had a predictable rhythm. When she wasn't waiting tables at the bar or staying late drinking, she was home smoking cigarettes and sipping her Southern Comfort in front of the television. Their apartment smelled of stale smoke and spilled drinks. The girl didn't mind her mother's slow descent into oblivion each night when it was just the two of them. Catherine could handle the canned soup and instant potatoes her mother dumped on the counter for their suppers. She could predict

Mother's moods, whether manic or depressed, and maneuver through her swings accordingly.

Elementary school was Catherine's anchor and sail. She memorized her way to straight A's and won every teacher's heart with her questions and focused intensity. Even in high school, with her home life completely disrupted, she had maintained her grades and made a path to scholarships and college. Of course, Mother and Baby June were long gone by then.

Mother had worked a steady job until she was pregnant with June. She had always managed to drag herself out of bed and get herself together with some coffee and makeup. Then she'd head down the steps to cross the wide gravel parking lot to the shabby restaurant-bar beside the highway. She waited tables, ran the cash register, and gabbed with her coworkers. That's where she met Steve.

Steve was a fun, loud guy, full of stories about his childhood in Louisiana. He began to show up at their second-story apartment every night that Mother didn't work and every night after work. He'd bring donuts for Catherine and a bottle of Southern Comfort for Mother. Catherine liked him well enough but had her suspicions about the treats.

"Hey, little lady, I found the chocolate ones with the white icing you like." He'd drop the bag into her lap and head back to the bedroom with the bottle. Mother would giggle, then laugh, then disappear into silence as the hours passed. Catherine would move into the kitchen where she could see the parking lot from her window. She did her homework and kept an eye out as Mother instructed. If it got really late, she fell asleep on the couch.

A few weeks after Steve had stopped showing up, Mother was sick during the day and stopped going into work. She stayed in bed or made her way to the couch where she'd smoke her cigarettes and hiss instructions.

"Catherine Hathaway, get your ass out of the chair or you'll miss the bus." She'd squeeze each vowel out through her nostrils, compressed and sharpened to jab the girl to action.

The donuts were long gone. Catherine and her mother were eating canned fruit and soup, potato flakes, and instant milk. Or at least she was. Her mother seemed to eat very little but drank her drinks every night. Her stomach had grown rounder and fuller, even as the cabinets had stayed empty.

The frigid bench numbed Catherine's backside. Her stomach churned although she'd eaten a solid breakfast of eggs and toast only an hour ago. The clay stayed molded to the shape of her soles, so she threw the useless stick and kicked off her shoes. She watched Percy skimming and sniffing along the fence. He glanced at her to see if she was headed inside yet.

"Patience, Percy. You'll get your treat when I get these shoes clean."

Placing them upside down in the grass, she adjusted the sprayer for maximum impact. She had to dislodge the imbedded muck now or the cold would turn it to rock. Digging it out would be impossible.

As a kid, Catherine hated the cold. She had only thin dresses and stockings with holes, wool coats with missing buttons, and mismatched hats and mittens. That winter when Mother was pregnant, the cold had squatted and settled outside the apartment building like a homeless man leaning heavy against their shabby door and windows. The iron railings along the steps punished her gloveless fingers. Oh, how those lean weeks had worn on—the weeks when Mother's shape and both of their worlds transformed.

Catherine remembered a particular cold night. Eight years old, she ran home from the bus stop, hurried up the iron stairs, and bustled into the apartment to shut out the bitter air and darkness.

"Mother, what are we having for dinner?" She rubbed her red, stinging hands together.

Her mother was a heap of blankets and pillows on the couch, exactly as Catherine had left her when she'd raced to the school bus that morning.

"I told you not to slam that damn door. Where have you been?" A muffled growl came from the frayed velour blanket pulled up past her mother's mouth.

"You know I have practice on Tuesday afternoons after school—"

"It's Tuesday?" It was more of a shriek than a question. "I need you to go to the neighbors' and borrow some potatoes or eggs or something for supper tonight. I haven't gotten money for groceries yet."

Catherine was horrified. "I can't beg for food!" It sounded like the whine of a five-year-old to her own ears.

Mother launched herself up and off of the couch, roused from languishing to lunging in seconds.

Catherine backed into the tiny kitchen, her spine stopped by the blunt edge of the counter.

"You can't have it both ways, Catherine Hathaway," Mother hissed into her face, her breath stale and dark. "If you want to eat, sometimes you have to swallow your pride."

Catherine shrank from her mother's hand poised by her face.

"Okay, I'll go." The words rushed out without inflection. "But who should I ask? And what should I say?"

Mother dropped her hand and lowered her voice. "Go to the Harpers. They're old, and they sometimes wave to me. Tell them I'm sick and can't work or go out."

In the weeks following, Catherine begged food from all of the surrounding apartments. Most of the neighbors gave what little they could spare, but some had no capacity for a handout.

"Tell your mother to get a job. And get a husband for that matter. You poor kids."

Poor kids? Catherine had dragged her feet along the frozen concrete walks and up the metal stairs. It dawned on her eight-year-old brain that Mother was pregnant. Definitely pregnant.

They were in trouble. The drinking was bad, and the shrinking food options were worse. Catherine remembered wondering about the rent and suspected Mother had gotten a check or two in the mail from relatives. Maybe even Steve. She didn't know. She never saw him again.

By the time the baby came, Catherine was begging regularly on the sidewalk in front of the shops beside the highway. Mother didn't know. The girl's pathetic yet clever signs, propped on her cardboard box, coaxed many to drop their coins and bills as they passed. At school she'd persuaded teachers to hire her for odd jobs like taping up old textbooks and cleaning the rabbit and lizard cages. She'd also been selling her note-taking skills to kids at school, letting them copy her work and teaching them memorization tricks. Plenty of classmates were willing to trade their spare change for her quick fixes. Catherine had become quite resourceful, learning to shop for food on a dime, organizing her world for survival and for the new mouth to feed.

A blue jay's shriek buzzed her eardrums. Catherine found herself a seventy-year-old woman, sitting on a bench, wet shoes in the grass and mud splatters on her clothing and toes. The atmosphere was heavy on her chest. She filled her lungs and grunted to stand. She'd leave the shoes and mud.

"I'll get to that mess another day." A headache tugged at the top of her head like a small cloud in a bright sky. "C'mon, Percy!" She made a megaphone with her hands. "Let's go!"

No dog. She whistled with two fingers between her teeth. He didn't show.

Percy was nowhere in the yard. Her chest tightened. She scanned along the fence on either side. She breathed with relief to see the gate was shut.

Still no dog. She whistled again then sang a shrill, "Treat, treat!"

A quiet *woof* came from behind her. She spun toward the back door. Percy stood on the top step, his eyes and ears a question mark.

"You scared me, you silly little mutt." His tail thumped against the wooden door. "Sorry for making you wait while I got lost in a faraway place."

She climbed the three short steps and followed Percy inside. Sliding into her fuzzy slippers, Catherine forgot all about Percy's muddy paws. The low-grade pain in her skull had settled in, threatening the better part of her day.

10. Percy and Arlo

Percy followed Catherine around the kitchen, his eyes locked on hers to see if she'd deliver the promised treat. He bounced, then crouched low by his bowl like a puppy ready to pounce, whining about how hungry he was from their walk. She laughed and said, "Okay, my little buddy, you win, even though I know you're not really hungry." She poured some kibble into his bowl. He finished it in less than ten seconds and ran back to the bag, begging for more.

"All done." Catherine's voice had an edge, which she instantly regretted. He lowered his ears and dropped his chin, eyes so sad she had to sit on her couch so he could scramble onto her lap. "C'mon, I'm sorry. Didn't mean to hurt your feelings."

Catherine thought Percy was the cutest little mutt in the world. Probably ugly to some, his compact twelve pounds of love and energy adorned her days. Like a pair of old leather shoes, his scent and texture embodied things an outsider would never understand. She woke each morning with him standing on her chest, wired with the excitement of a toddler. *Why are we still in bed?* They ended each day huddled together, his body conforming to the curve of her back.

Percy softened the effects of each annoying reminder of her age and imperfections. Even when he lunged at other dogs while walking on a leash in the neighborhood, she chose her soft-focus lens. Her love for him was nearsighted, if not blind, like a parent's view that their undisciplined kid is somehow cute.

Catherine loved the little dog more than she wanted to. "Heartache waiting to happen" was her tagline for every pet that had come and gone through her life. Caring for another creature cost her a lot in time and trouble. Percy's dirt aggravated her pain as she bent again and again to clean his paws, his spills, his messes. But he paid her back with more love than she deserved. And unlike some of the humans she'd known, he accepted her silences without taking them personally.

Percy never noticed her obsessive habits either— the constant worrying about the weather, her particular way of stacking glassware and plastic containers, the piles of old newspapers waiting to be read. He didn't see her check, recheck, then check again her account balance against the bank's statements every month. When Catherine gathered tiny pieces of leaves and lint from her otherwise spotless floors, Percy just rolled over and went back to sleep.

He had some obsessive habits of his own. Like licking his paws nonstop, mesmerized by the monotony of the sound and motion. Also, he rolled in every patch of disgusting detritus his nose exposed in the woods. And he was known to destroy a flower bed in relentless pursuit of a mole. Not to mention he'd begun snoring loudly throughout the night like her other dog had before he died.

Arlo, her black lab, was graying and arthritic when she'd discovered the lump nestled behind his front leg. His suffering hadn't shown at first. Like a child whose "normal" is whatever is happening, he endured the slow burn of his disease for months. Because he had nothing to compare it to, he had no complaints. But as the tumor grew, so did his discomfort. It fell to Catherine to decide when Arlo's life should end. The dog was in bad shape by the time she made the appointment. She struggled to lift him into the car to take him to the vet. The nurse cried with her as Catherine stroked his trusting old face. The drugs did their duty, and Arlo was gone for good.

For months after, she'd find his stiff black hairs woven into the couch's upholstery and clinging to her clothing. She'd even found one stuck to the butter dish in the refrigerator. She didn't miss his mess. But these little reminders lodged in her heart, felt like his way of staying. His way of saying, *Don't forget me.*

She left her half-duplex home soon after and moved on from Arlo, her closest companion of nearly fourteen years—like she had eventually moved on from all the people in her life. The older she got, the less she wanted to invest in relationships, hard as they were for her in the first place. She shed colleagues and acquaintances like a dog drops its fur. The few friends remaining when she retired had drifted away like fish let off the hook. They disappeared into her murky past, in part from mutual lack of interest.

On the bright side, moving to her new place held the promise of starting over. The spaces were easier to keep clean without dogs and people. The time was all hers to manage. No more hours spent preparing homemade dog food or taking the dog for walks each morning and evening. No need for stocking the cabinets with crackers and cookies in case someone stopped by. The quiet was as quiet as she could ever remember. After Arlo died, she resolved, "No more pets. I'll grow old alone."

The ladies were agreeable.

Miss Catherine, taking care of yourself is hard enough, let alone loving another needy creature.

Old Woman, no one needs the heartache. Would've been better to have never loved at all.

But with old and alone had come the kind of loneliness that squeezes out determination. And the ladies' opinions. It took her a few years of retirement and utter isolation to admit that her old-age resolution was not going to stick. She'd found Percy as a puppy in a rescue shelter, and it was love at first lick.

11. God on the Lawn

The crepe myrtle looked dead. Catherine twisted the tip of a branch. She broke off the brittle twig and concealed it in her palm—unable to bring herself to look for green inside.

She had neglected the slender tree this year, forgetting to feed and water it, tucked away as it was between the gate and a wall. Two years ago she planted the sapling at the side of the house, the end of her walkway. Last year new growth showed up in late spring and waited until summer to grace her walk with vivacious pink buds. Later still the buds burst into tiny magenta bouquets. They displayed such glory then: waving like hands in a congregation of praise, the gratitude of a tree coming back to life.

Not that Catherine had ever been part of such a congregation. Any praise-gatherings she attended were proper conservative church services, sedate and civil. Hands in the air would disrupt the peace. She kept hers resting on her lap, where they couldn't pressure the undemonstrative into guilt for their stillness or prompt agnostics to make a mockery with their pretense. Plus it just wasn't natural. Didn't matter anyway. She could not remember the last time she went to church.

Catherine preferred to worship in her backyard garden beneath a stately oak.

A tree that looks at God all day and lifts her leafy arms to pray.

This was her kind of church: let the birds and trees extend unselfconscious gratitude to the one who made them.

Lift her hands with the branches? Sometimes. But she rarely sang with the birds in their joy of being alive. No, not on days when old age rendered her cursing and complaining to her maker, the one who allowed her life to unravel as it had. God could have made matters easier, better. Instead, he let confusion and loneliness become the bookends of her seven decades. Adventures in anguish and grief filled the space between.

Gee, thanks for the invitation to your pity party, Old Woman.

Miss Catherine, only God knows how you've suffered.

A chill dampened her Sunday morning. Catherine tilted her face to the sky, hugging her heavy coat close and soaking up the sun's spare heat. Percy deserted her to poke around on the far side of the house. A faint wind changed direction, sending church bells shimmering her way. They rippled through her layers of rough coverings, stirring her like a tremor in the earth. She warmed to the subtle shift that words couldn't touch. Her hands tingled with a quicker pulse.

Arms at her side, she strolled to her favorite bench and sat down.

Growing up in the South, the girl Catherine had absorbed a detached and vague kinship with God, untaught and uncertain about his direct relation to her. Mother had no communication with God except her curses in his name. She taught her daughter no specific religious position save that Religion was the disease driving people to keep people like Mother and her at arm's length.

Catherine was a mongrel born of a mongrel when it came to pedigrees of faith. She learned that Mother's lineage contained a great-great somebody who was a solid Christian pastor or preacher. But the trickle-down effect diluted any honest faith she may have inherited. Mother's family were like ghosts, haunting the spoken and unspoken oaths that hovered on her mother's lips and throughout young Catherine's life. By default, she was an outcast like her mother. Close relatives disowned them both. The rare Christmas gifts or guilty checks in the mail were godsends or windfalls, depending on how you looked at it.

Mother despised her family either way. Father's family wanted nothing to do with Mother or her child. Maybe they didn't realize Catherine existed. She wasn't sure. Mother wouldn't say. Regardless, the familial ties disintegrated in their disuse, leaving the mother and girl virtual orphans.

Catherine's school friends intrigued her with their descriptions of church attendance and Sunday school lessons. Their mysterious God club stirred her curiosity. They invited her along once or twice, but Mother would not allow it. And so Catherine's creator defaulted to absent father. She regarded him wistfully or accusingly, depending on the day. On occasion, he resembled a kindly grandfather she hoped to meet one day.

Once, after a friend described her prayers to the Lord, young Catherine decided to give it a try. For weeks as an eight-year-old, she spoke to him every night. Eyes on the bedroom ceiling, hands folded under her chin, she'd tell the Almighty what she needed and ask what he would do.

"Dear God, will you help me with my math like you helped my friend Annie with her spelling test?"

"Dear God, can you make me stop growing so the boys don't tease me all the time?"

"Dear God, are you really out there?"

She waited. Her stomach rumbled. A muffled television boomed through the wall. The scary neighbor lady shouted two doors down. God's voice remained muted, his message muddled and mysterious. Without obvious answers to her simple prayers, the girl put her search on hold. She held on to the image of a God-out-there-somewhere, hoping he'd show up later in life.

Now, in her old age, in her new haven, Catherine began to look and listen for him again. This time, she expected no audible voice. She didn't look for him in every favorable turn of circumstances. Didn't search for divinity in the people who pressed pamphlets into her palm. Couldn't imagine that people in the pews had a relational advantage. Nor did she think she heard the Spirit when it was just the ladies' rancor filling her head. She wished for no special deliveries, no secret notes behind the bookcase, no personal messages between the lines in a storybook.

She invited him instead to the secluded places of her mind, the empty spaces between breaths. Moments when the ladies were silent and Mother didn't intrude, rare as those moments were. Catherine met with God on the lawn. She searched for his face in her flowers, strained to hear his voice in the trees, and even sought him in the flow of her days.

Her faith was primitive, a crude altar to the awesome God of creation, revealed in more than his glorious plants and animals. No, she did not think every butterfly and bird deserved her worship. But both her cultivated garden and her untamed surroundings spoke of a Magnificence and Power deserving her reverence.

Her heart held the tales of God's love and redemption in a tentative embrace, resonating with the story of a sacrifice that set people free. With hope she imagined his touch of healing and forgiveness. With certainty she wrapped her head around the ideas of mercy and grace. The best ideas the world had going. She just didn't know how to sift and shuffle them through her old gray head to the blood red flow of life in real time.

Catherine did know that her best days were bare feet on the lawn. The voices of chickadees and nuthatches tuned to the creek's musical chortling spoke volumes to her soul. When the wild wooded paths whispered of hidden dangers and the front door opened to chaos and decay, her world behind the wooden walls, beneath the arching sky, brushed up against her like the mingled breath of a mother and infant. The Spirit of God might be an invisible wind streaming along the surface of the creek, rising to fill her nostrils with fragrances from a distant land. Or it breathed in the tangible love of her dog. Perhaps it glowed in every graceful glory in between.

A gray squirrel scrambled along an oak's high branch. Catherine stretched her neck to follow its scrabbling ascent. Effortless and fearless, it left the limits of its dwindling branch and leaped across space in graceful suspense. For less than a second, the common rodent transformed into a spectacular singularity. It landed on a solid limb and clambered down the other side of the tree.

Percy returned and leaned his body against her heavy leather boots. Catherine curled her toes inside thick socks to buffer the chill. She tucked one hand into a deep pocket. Her other clasped the crepe myrtle twig, concealing death or restoration. She would let it take its time to tell.

Closeness to God was more an idea than a feeling, more a longing than a fulfillment. But someday, if she believed what people said, she hoped to follow on his heels along the hidden paths that stretched beyond her homemade heaven.

12. Appearances

The rain came and stayed for three days. Now that the clouds were clearing, Catherine pressed her garage door opener to let in some fresh air. Time to sift through some old boxes and rid herself of accumulated junk. If she could part with her old college textbooks, obsolete teaching curricula, and whatever else lay buried, maybe she'd find room in the stable for her old Subaru, left standing outside all these years.

From the shadows at the edge of her garage, she spied the new neighbor attempting to get out of her car. First she slid her knees sideways from beneath the steering wheel. Then she grabbed the top of the open car door to heave herself up from the seat, wincing as she moved. Steadying her bulk between door and roof, the woman stood there as if waiting for something to settle. The top layer of her hair was an unflattering shade of turquoise-blue. For someone no more than thirty years old, she seemed to be in a lot of pain.

The woman leaned to lift a clump of plastic grocery bags from the passenger seat and let out a loud groan. Catherine considered disappearing back into her garage and getting on with her work. Instead, she stepped into her driveway.

May as well find out what we're dealing with and be a neighbor of sorts.

A cloud's shadow fled. Sunlight spilled across the cement. She lifted and dropped the heavy lid of her plastic trash can. The young woman looked at her for a split second, then turned away with half a wave.

"Hello." Catherine's voice was loud but neutral.

The woman turned toward her again, her eyes angled sideways and several plastic bags clutched in her right hand. She shrugged, as if in apology, then spoke in a slow drone. "Oh, hey, hi. I'm, uh, we just moved in a month or two ago." She lifted the last words up like a question.

"Yes, your daughter came by," Catherine called across the gap between them.

The woman called back, her gaze as high as Catherine's knees now, her voice still flat, "Oh, yeah, I'm so sorry. She can be a bit much, and I can't—she doesn't always do what I tell her to do. I'll make sure she doesn't come over and bother you again."

"Oh. It's not a big problem, really." Catherine moved a few steps closer. "She's fine, very . . . energetic."

Energetic? More like belligerent! She should teach the kid to obey.

Not a problem? More like a terror. That child is the definition of trouble.

The young woman's eyes finally met hers. "Yes, she can be a handful." Her expression was blank.

"And her brother, he's my little helper. But he sometimes forgets to watch her." The woman rolled her eyes. "I'll talk to him about that. I'm sorry to be a bother." She studied the ground again.

"Well, my name is Catherine Hathaway. Welcome to the neighborhood." Catherine forced a smile, covering the distance between their driveways and extending her hand.

Old Woman, you've gone too far. What happened to keeping to yourself?

Miss Hathaway, a smile will only encourage her to look for a handout.

"I'm Patty," said the mother, coming forward to shake Catherine's hand. As she took a step, one of her plastic bags split open and dumped its load in the driveway. Before Catherine could say anything, the young woman let out an enraged shriek and released the other bags to the ground. Bringing her hands to her head, she stared down at the pile of cans and boxes as if they were her betrayers.

Catherine froze like a mouse cornered by a cat. She stared at the woman who was beside herself in the driveway stomping her foot like a child. Finally, she said, "Let me help."

She took two quick steps to steady the woman whose legs were now wobbling. Nearly a foot taller than Patty, Catherine had to stoop to support her left elbow as the woman bent to gather the food. Instead of lifting the bags, Patty collapsed to sitting in the middle of her groceries. Face flushed, she let out a strangled laugh.

"I'm so sorry—what a mess. Why do things like this happen to me? And now here you are seeing what a mess I am . . ." Catherine nodded without thinking. Patty burbled on. "But I'll get the kids to help me pick up this stuff. Don't you worry about it."

"It's just a bag of groceries." Catherine bent beside her and touched one of her shoulders. "Let me get you a new bag or two." She straightened her knees and hurried back toward her garage. Behind her, she heard the woman screaming for her children. She seemed a little crazy. Was she drunk?

"Patrick, Tazzy, get out here and help me with this mess! Patrick, get your butt out here and help me with the groceries! Patrick, Paaahtrick!"

When Catherine returned with her handful of cloth bags, the boy had already gotten his mother to standing. She was leaning on him and wheezing. He spoke quietly to her and wiped her face with his sleeve. Catherine piled cans and boxes into one of her bags. Straightening to face them, she found no words to soften their awkward positions.

The mother shuddered as if coming out of a daze. "Okay, I'm fine, Patrick—I'm fine! Grab that can from under the car." She pushed his hand away from her face. "The neighbors must think I'm a crazy person." The pitch of her voice rose. She glanced at the road, then at Catherine looming over her.

The boy came back with the can, placed it carefully in the bag, and took it from Catherine. He peered up at her from under his overgrown blond bangs, then looked to his mother.

Patty said, "Oh, oh yeah, this is our next-door neighbor. Um, Cathy Hathaway."

"It's Catherine Hathaway, actually." She nodded, surprised by her relaxed tone.

Flashing a bright smile, the boy shifted the bag to his left hand and reached his right toward her. "Pleased to meet you, Miss Catherine. I'm Patrick."

Winter

*The greatest sources of our sufferings
are the lies we tell ourselves.*

—Elvin Semrad

*...the wind sprang up afresh, with a kind of bitter
song, as if it said: 'This is reality, whether you like it or
not. All those frivolities of summer, the light and
shadow, the living mask of green that trembled over
everything, they were lies, and this is what was
underneath. This is the truth.*

—Willa Cather, *My Ántonia*

13. The Program

*C*atherine Hathaway, get in here and pick up that crying baby.

Catherine had dozed off on her couch in the middle of the day. She'd been dreaming of Baby June, until Percy, yapping at a turkey vulture lurking in the tree outside, startled her awake. His bark began as Mother's voice in her dream, a sound that always cut through her reveries, even when the baby's cries did not.

Catherine sat up and stared at the wall without seeing. Oh, how she loved her baby sister, June. Nine years apart, Catherine was more like a mom to her than a sister. Especially in those early days when June was a newborn. Mother was either sleeping or gone. They had moved to a new place in a scarier part of town, an apartment smaller and more cramped than the last one. It was farther from civilization but had a small patch of trees and a trickling stream behind the shabby two-story building.

Her school hadn't changed, but the new bus carried an entirely different set of kids, kids she didn't know and who didn't want to know her. Mother was back to working part time at a different restaurant-bar down the road. She often stayed late to drink or go home with someone she'd met during her shift. A neighbor lady ran a haphazard daycare in the untidy apartment below theirs. That's where Baby June went when necessary.

"You get her as soon as you get home from school if I'm not here, Catherine. Can't afford to pay that woman for barely watching my kid."

When Mother was home and sober, Catherine used those moments to fly out the door and explore the depths of the woods and stream. Some of the teenagers from the complex had carved out rough trails just past the edge of the buildings. They'd hover under the trees, drinking and smoking and calling out to her as she passed. Middle-schooler Catherine always steered clear of the big kids and their heaps of cheap bottles and scattered plastic wrappers. She skirted the rain-battered clumps of yellow grass matted with pulpy trash. Farther into the woods, some of the younger kids had made forts out of cardboard and wooden pallets, places to play and escape their slum-like dwellings. She would duck her head into some of their nooks before heading into the deeper reaches of the woods—hidden spots that others hadn't bothered to explore and where the trash hadn't yet drifted.

She found her place apart, her escape from the worries of home and school. Catherine's sanctuary was a small cluster of pines beside the tiny creek. This group of petite evergreens huddled and leaned to one side where the wind had urged them and where and the creek had drawn them with promises of steady sustenance. She'd settle in for an hour at most, toes in the stream, knowing Mother would notice her absence when dinner time loomed and the job or the booze stirred her to move in its direction.

That particular day Catherine arrived home in near dark. Baby June's cries reached her from the other side of the door. Mother grabbed her hard the minute she stepped into the dim, sour-smelling apartment. Her arm stinging with the fingernail marks and her face hot with tears, Catherine ran to gather up the sweaty-headed infant from the tiny crib in the bedroom they all shared. Her chapped-face sister on her hip, she started supper with a box of macaroni and the cheapest hot dogs anyone could buy. Turning the electric burner to high, she set the pot of cold water on the black coil to await its orange glow.

A knock made her jump.

Mother shouted from the couch, a cigarette bouncing between her lips. "Catherine, get the door. And tell them we don't want any or we don't have any. I've got a headache if it's the fat lady from across the way peddling her homemade jewelry."

Catherine, baby in arms, twisted the knob to peek outside. A woman and a man, both nicely dressed, smiled at her.

"Hello, young lady. We're from Child Protective Services. Can we come in for a quick conversation?"

She didn't know what Child Protective Services was or why she should say no to such nice-looking people. She automatically opened the door wide and stepped aside to let them in. Curses flew from the couch.

They stood stiffly inside the door, engulfed in a cloud of cigarette smoke, and looked about the place. Mother had disappeared into the bedroom. But they had all seen the back of her matted cream-colored bathrobe whisking around the side of the door frame.

"Ma'am? Ma'am," they called down the hall. "We need to talk to you. Please. We're here to ask you a few questions and offer some help if you need it."

"Don't need it—now get out of my home," came her muffled shout from the bedroom.

"We've had a report about your children, and we just need follow up. We won't stay long. Please come out and hear what we have to say."

Her puffy face appeared from behind the door frame. She slid a shoulder, hip, and leg out so that exactly one half of her showed. Catherine wanted to laugh at her strange presentation. She bounced Baby June instead, who cried louder and reached for her mom.

"What'd you do now, Catherine? Steal some money from a kid at school or convince someone to pay you for doing their homework?"

Mother was rumpled—and slightly drunk. Catherine kept her eyes on the two adults standing there, one with a vinyl briefcase and both with plastic smiles. Mother had moved closer to them in the hallway now, leaning her lanky frame against the wall for support.

"No, ma'am, not a school thing. An anonymous caller to our offices said they'd seen some kids here showing signs of neglect. A baby and an older girl."

"What the hell? Who has the right to make an anonymous call and accuse me of neglect? You have no right to try and take my kids from me." Her indignation and anger hung in the stale air between them.

"No one wants to take your children, Mrs. . . ." He raised his eyebrows. "We only want to make sure they're being taken care of."

Catherine realized her mother was about to do that move in which she'd tuck in her chin, rise as tall as possible, open her arms wide, fake a smile, and say things like, *Do I look like the kind of woman who would* . . . Fill in the blank. It didn't matter. The question and the pose always threw people off guard and sent them backpedaling. Anyone could sense she was a simmering pot about to boil over.

Catherine rushed into the space between Mother in the hallway and the people in the living room. She held out the baby. "Mommy, Baby June is so glad you're feeling better after how sick you've been lately. Here, she wants you to hold her."

Mother's lips puckered, her eyebrows stitched in a tight frown. Half a second later, she moved to grab the baby and cuddle and coo over her in her most maternal tones. Catherine scooted back into the kitchen, stirred the macaroni into the boiling water, and turned the burner to low.

The CPS man dropped his hands to his side. "Look, we're not here to accuse anyone or take your kids away. But we have to investigate every call we get. Seems like everybody's doing okay here. Anything you want to tell us?" He glanced at Catherine, whose face showed no signs of her recent tears. She hugged herself, covering the marks on her arm.

The young woman glanced sideways at her partner, took a quick look at Catherine in the kitchen, then checked her watch.

"Well, yes." Mother stepped toward the living room, bouncing June. "I have been sick. I'm a single mother, and it's hard to be working and taking care of my two sweet girls. Catherine sometimes has to pick up the slack. But I'm much better now, and I appreciate you checking on us, Mr. . . ."

"Wallace. And this is Miss Baker."

"I'm Carla Hathaway. Pleased to meet you. I know you're just doing your job." She had expanded herself in the hallway like a confident peacock.

Catherine stared at Miss Baker's pretty hair and her matching skirt and blazer. The young woman shifted on her high heels. "Mrs. Hathaway, there are many resources for moms—people—in need of help from time to time. Food vouchers and classes for parenting and—"

"Terrific, I will check that out. Leave me a few pamphlets and forms I can look over, thanks."

Catherine followed the two visitors outside and watched them plod down the concrete steps from the second-floor apartments to the parking lot. The sun had set. The lamp in the lot glinted off the windshield of their car as they backed out and away from her.

The woman smiled and waved from the passenger side; the girl lifted her hand halfway then let it fall back to her side. She returned to find Mother on the couch feeding Baby June her bottle, both framed in the doorway like a storybook picture. Her mother seemed suddenly old and sad. She looked up when Catherine clicked the door shut behind, her face sagging and flushed. Catherine braced for it, but the tongue-lashing didn't come.

"Let's order a pizza for supper tonight, why don't we?" Mother's voice was high and tight. She stood, handed the baby to Catherine, turned off the burner, and brushed by her into the bedroom. The girl wondered what their visitors would've thought if they'd discovered the empty liquor bottles in the trash, if they'd looked inside the empty refrigerator, if they'd inspected that old crib with its rickety legs and cracked plastic mattress. If they'd known how sick Baby June got sometimes. But they had barely moved from the doorway. What could they have done to make things better anyway? The situation was not so bad. Not as bad as it could be. Would be.

As a nine-year-old, had she thought to raise an alarm? Why had she rushed to cover her mother's failings? Catherine could not remember.

You can't have it both ways, Catherine Hathaway. Either get with the program or get out of the way.

Mother didn't say it at the time, but Catherine heard it now as she hunched on the couch, massaging small circles on her temples. The dream and the memory resolved into a single low-grade hum, the throbbing in her skull a new normal. Rising, she marveled at how well she had learned to get with the program.

14. Residue

Shaking off the nap's residue, Catherine joined Percy at the window. A hulking black turkey vulture lifted from a low branch in the oak halfway down her yard. Grabbing a jacket and opening the back door, she followed the dog outside. He ran barking beneath the bird's fleeing shadow, thinking he had done the evicting, when, indeed, the vulture had already decided to move on.

Catherine shuddered, her thin black jacket no match for the bitter winter wind. The cozy warmth of the house had lulled her into a dull forgetfulness of how cold the days were getting. She could barely remember what summer felt like.

How funny, she thought. In summer the cold is hard to imagine. Yet in winter, the hot days are difficult to recall—except for the ones constantly springing to the surface of her memory like sweat breaking out on her scalp, days that live like a sticky residue on her skin. Catherine watched Percy dart along the creek, and her mind skipped backwards.

One humid summer day when Baby June was just a newborn, the radio was on in the kitchen, playing in the background. The heat in the apartment was killing the three of them, but Mother said they couldn't afford to turn on the air-conditioning.

"Go outside with the baby, Catherine. Take her to the playground while I take a nap."

The playground was an assemblage of rusty, squeaking things that the creepy kids had taken over for the summer. It was no place for a girl and a baby.

"Mother, I can't go up there. Too many older kids around and nothing to do."

Mother snapped. "Catherine Hathaway, you can't have your cake and eat it too. Now go outside and play with the baby."

The girl Catherine was only nine and didn't know what cake had to do with anything, especially since she hadn't eaten any cake in months.

"No," she said. A flash of pain immediately seared her cheek and bounced the side of her head against the wall. When Catherine opened her eyes, Mother's hand slipped back into her bathrobe pocket. Catherine remembered touching her throbbing face and choking back tears while Baby June cried on and on and on. Mother turned and walked into the bedroom.

That was the first time it happened. It happened only a handful of times after that. Just a handful.

On a few occasions, Mother had slapped her when she'd let the door slam behind her. Once, Catherine rushed inside to ask for money for the ice cream truck. Her mother had whirled from the sink, backhanded her across the cheek, and shrieked, "How many times have I told you, don't let the door slam? Damn it, Catherine." Mother dropped her head, shaking and facing the sink again. Her remorse resulted in homemade pancakes for lunch, but she never dished out an apology. Perhaps she knew she'd do it again.

The next time Catherine forgot to catch the door before it crashed against its frame, Mother had trekked from the bedroom in a drunken rage. Her aim was off, but her hand was a fist. She landed it on her daughter's chin before collapsing to the couch. She slept it off, never knowing what she'd done, never asking about the bruise on Catherine's chin.

Percy chased a chipmunk. It ducked into a tiny hole near the fence, chirping in panicked zeal. Its disappearance left him confounded and confused. His nose had betrayed him. He circled and sniffed, but the rodent's smell had evaporated.

The heavy memories pressed Catherine into a patio chair, her heart pounding and her face hot. The light had changed, and the wind picked up. She leaned her forehead on her palm, elbow propped on a knee. As the air pressure shifted, her ears clicked, and the headache ticked up a notch. A storm was coming in.

Above her, treetops churned in invisible currents. Above them, turkey vultures took advantage of the free ride. A cold raindrop splashed down the back of her neck, sending a shiver that reached her core. She stood and laid a hand on her burning-cold cheek. The closest oaks bent their heads to report. She should go inside.

She stood and whistled for Percy. Stumbling, she headed for the steps.

15. Invasion

"Hey, I saw you fall down!" A tiny voice pierced the haze in Catherine's head.

She came to her senses like waking from a deep sleep. Dropped down in the middle of she-didn't-know-where, without a past or possibly even a future, for nearly ten seconds she was pure awareness. Not a single thought passed through her mind. What she was, let alone who she was, were questions she had yet to ask.

What did register was the rough stone kissing her cheek, the tilted dark outline of her fence, and the scent of wet earth soaking her nostrils. She was lying on the ground.

A hawk's eerie cry filtered down from high above. A metallic tingle on her tongue told her she was indeed alive. Catherine recognized the knobby hands that pressed to lift her twisted torso from the rain-splattered patio.

What happened? The wind was hissing in the trees lining the creek. Her back reported its distress in a primitive part of her brain. With a groan, she rolled to her rear end and let the dismal rainy view sink in.

"I saw you fall down!" The loud little voice entered her atmosphere again. Blinking, she discovered the wide-eyed neighbor girl just a few feet away. Percy growled and wagged his tail, moving toward the wild-looking child, then scuttling from her.

Ah yes, it came to Catherine: she had been climbing the back steps into her house. The gate's squeak and Percy's bark coincided with her tripping on the first step. The last thing she remembered was the thrust of a rough plank along her palms and the clunk of her forehead on wood. She must have lost consciousness and tumbled sideways down the steps.

"Why did you fall down?" The kid was closer now, staring at Catherine as if encountering a ghost. Her thin pink nightgown fluttered around her ankles. Blue eyes and tiny ears poked through straggly hair. She screamed, "I see blood!"

Catherine moved a hand to her forehead, finding it mostly intact. Just a tiny bump where she'd hit the landing. Drops of blood painted her fingertips. Her tongue probed the shredded flesh inside her cheek.

Still sitting, she wiped her fingers on her trousers and glared at the little girl.

"It's all right, just a scrape." Her voice wobbled. She cleared her throat. "What are you doing in my yard? How did you get in here?"

"Through there." The girl pointed behind her. The gate was wide open.

Percy had decided she was a friend and was now licking a scab on her knee. She reached a finger to touch his nose. "I came to pet your dog and I saw you fall down."

Catherine frowned. She had forgotten to latch it again.

She rolled to her knees, stood with a wince, and tottered a few steps to the bench. Leaning her thighs against the back, she stared at the little girl kneeling in the grass. Percy licked her fingers while the girl alternately jerked her hands away then offered them again. Her eyes jumped to Catherine. "He likes me."

Catherine swayed her way back to the steps and clung to the railing. "Yes, he likes you. But I didn't invite you in here." She brushed a clump of hair away from her face and touched her forehead again.

The little girl gaped up at her with wide eyes above red and swollen cheeks. Catherine moved to get a closer look. The girl stood abruptly and scuffled backward a few steps.

Catherine halted, folding her arms on her chest. Her long black coat loosened and billowed out behind her. "Okay, go home now, little girl." She tried to sound lighthearted, but it came out heavy-handed. "And don't come into my garden again."

"You need a boo-boo sticker. I have some at my house." The child stood straight as a poplar tree, holding her ground. Facing Catherine, she had squared her hips, planted her feet, and placed her arms on her chest,

"Thank you, but I have bandages of my own. Now go home." She sharpened her voice, sending it through the space between them like an arrow.

"Why?" The child was shivering and seemed ready to cry. Her hands turned to fists.

"Because it's my private property, and you didn't knock. Now go!" Her coat ballooned open as she pointed her bony arm. Her gray cotton trousers whipped around her legs like sheets caught on tree limbs.

"Are you the bad witch right now?" The child's chin trembled, her voice a pinched whine.

Catherine's hands fell to her side. "What? I'm not—"

"I have boo-boo stickers at my house!" The girl was shouting as if Catherine were deaf. She scooted backward toward the gate.

"I know. I have them too, so go home!" She returned the shout, her arms drooping on her frame.

The girl had loosened her fists, but her shoulders held tight, nearly touching her ears. Her elvish features were set like stone. Red scabby lines striped her left forearm where her pink sleeve rode up.

Catherine's throat tightened. A wave of dizziness threatened her balance. She lurched to the bench again and plopped to sitting, head bowed and hair draping her face. She focused on her two big toes poking out of holes in her canvas sneakers and the tattered hem of the coat she should have tossed years ago. She must look like a wild woman who had wandered in from the forest.

Her hands clamped the edge of the bench. She could have really hurt herself. What if she had done more damage to her head? She lifted her chin. What if the kid hadn't come looking for Percy? How long would she have lain there in the rain? Sighing, she turned and fixed her gaze on the shivering child in her yard.

"Yes, go get me a boo-boo sticker." Her bark sent the little creature scurrying through the gate.

Catherine touched her wound again, a small scab already formed.

Well, at least you were smart enough to catch yourself and not crack your head wide open, Old Woman.

You could have really gotten hurt. This falling thing had better not be a trend.

It'll pass. Just a little scrape, you dummy. Go inside before more people come to see the crazy old lady.

Miss Catherine, don't forget to shut that gate.

She grunted as she pawed the ground for her stick and straightened her knees. She marched to the gate, and with her slam, the pine boards rattled on impact.

Back at her kitchen table, Catherine examined her palms while Percy trolled the floor for crumbs. The furnace murmured on. She shivered as sweat surfaced on her forehead. When she dropped her hand to stroke Percy, he licked at the blood on her fingers. Catherine pushed him away. A little bump wasn't going to ruin her day.

There was a bigger problem to consider: the invasion. That kid didn't know her haven was off limits—yet.

Bad witch, ha! Such a brat. She doesn't even know how to act. Trespassing and saying what's what with that grimy little face.

She's such a lonely little scaredy-cat. And those scratches on her arm . . .

Probably fights with her brother and gets what she deserves. Hasn't learned to get with the program yet.

The ladies conversation faded as a thin bright light filtered through an opening in Catherine's mind. An idea formed: she could let the girl in from time to time. Hadn't she been wide-eyed and precocious herself once? Hadn't she cared for little kids not so many years ago? Where had her tenderness gone?

Although she'd struggled as a young teacher, she grew to love engaging the kids in the study of living things, the joys of life in the natural world.

"Look at this butterfly. Do you know where it came from? Touch this moss. Can you believe how soft it is?"

They were all ears and eyes, her kindergarteners, and later, fifth-graders. She missed them sometimes. They wouldn't recognize her now.

Catherine laughed out loud.

"You're losing it, Hathaway. You wouldn't recognize them either, because they're grown up and have kids of their own."

Since her retirement, the distance between her first years of teaching and the kids throughout her career had shrunk to a small paragraph, a general summary of events in her memory. She used to recall each student by name, could place them in the time frame they were hers. Now, whenever she tried to divide up the years, the faces, they stayed compressed like particle board, compact layers too thick and heavy to dissect.

Her instinct to hide this loss of perspective had added to her desire to hide from people. With colleagues at school, she'd kept a professional distance anyway, allowing few interlopers into her kingdom of solitude and control.

But this was new, this rigidity seeping into her bones and muscles, tightening around her chest, climbing her spine, and threatening her brain. A petrified tree in process. She feared its final stage.

Percy barked and Catherine shuddered. She stood to scoop a cup of food into his bowl. He scarfed up every nugget, and she swept the floor. Her bright idea faded away. The ladies returned to center stage.

Miss Catherine, you've earned the right to be left alone. You survived a lonely childhood.

You don't even know if the kid's lonely, Old Woman. Besides, she'd mess up the yard and get in the way.

Privacy is important. It should be obvious to that little invader.

Yes, you may as well get good at being a bad witch.

Catherine's wound throbbed. She checked it in the mirror. A large greenish egg protruded from her forehead. Fishing an ice pack from the freezer, she pressed it against her head. No going soft now. She must take action.

"I'll find a way to make my boundaries clearer," she said to Percy. He circled a cushion, preparing for another nap.

16. The Stakes

Catherine was up with the birds. Today was a day of purpose. The solution came to her this morning: reinforcements in the form of wooden stakes. She would line them up along the property line and leave no room for the renters to guess where their front yard ended and hers began. Maybe blocking the way to her path and gate would abolish the invitation to invade. If that Patty woman asked, she'd explain they were for supporting her tomatoes in the spring. But the new boundary would speak for itself. Perhaps Patty would get a clue and keep her kids to herself.

It was much too early for tomatoes, of course. But by spring her indoor seedlings would be ready for these sunny spots in the front. She was, after all, just getting a jump on the season.

In her heavy wool jacket, Catherine fumbled with frozen fingers in the garage. Where were those stakes? She kicked aside a cardboard box. They were here somewhere. Probably behind Mother's junk. "Some inheritance *that* turned out to be."

She spied the red metal toolbox and remembered her mother's hammer entombed inside. Unlatching the lid, she discovered again the few tools her mother had left her: a dull gray padlock, the wooden-handled hammer, and a couple of screwdrivers in the top tray. Various nails, bolts, and screws rolled in the rusty bottom.

The superintendent from Mother's last apartment had contacted Catherine all those years ago, asking if she wanted the things her mother had left behind. His call had shocked her. Last she'd heard, her mother was homeless. Catherine was surprised she'd recovered enough to rent a place and stunned that she'd had Catherine's number.

Still in college, Catherine had asked him to store the stuff until she could collect it. After graduating with her teaching degree, she made the trip back to her hometown, hoping for clues about what Mother had been doing and where she had gone.

The man who'd called knew nothing of Mother's whereabouts.

"I hardly ever saw her going in or out of the apartment. I didn't know she was gone until the lady in the place below hers complained of a leaky ceiling." He found no furniture, only a dripping toilet. And the tools plus a few boxes. Mother had scrawled Catherine's name and dormitory phone number across a cardboard flap.

Her leftovers had disappointed Catherine once more. No forwarding address or personal note. Only a bunch of useless tools, musty books, and random blankets and clothing.

The stench of standing water reached her from somewhere in the dank garage. Catherine rolled her eyes and sighed. "One more thing to take care of." She grabbed the hammer, slammed the lid shut, and pushed the button for the automatic door. The brisk winter air swept through her lungs like a stiff broom. She scooted outside, smiling in the bold and brilliant sunlight. A crow flew close overhead, calling his cronies to join him as he descended on a small dead animal in the road.

A door slammed. Catherine's head jerked toward the house beside hers where a small someone had emerged. She squinted. It was that little invader who appeared inside her gate a few days ago. She never did return with that bandage. Not surprising.

The little girl stared from her porch, her eyes red and puffy, a shiny streak below her nose.

"Hey what're you doing?" She called to Catherine in a loud, nasally voice.

"Stuff," Catherine called back, holding her gaze.

The child hopped down her front steps and continued hopping across her driveway and through the muddy grass between them. She hovered on the edge of Catherine's yard, her stiff, puffy coat unzipped, a bright red scarf dangling halfway off of her neck.

"I'm doing stuff too." The girl watched as Catherine pounded a stake into the hard earth. The kid wiped her dripping nose with the sleeve of her coat. A string of hair had pasted itself to the side of her face. Catherine raised her head and one eyebrow, resisting the urge to move toward the child and dislodge the sticky strand.

"I'm five." The girl stood beside her now, still shouting and forgetting whatever it was that had made her cry inside.

"Good for you." Catherine said, wanting to shout back to make a point. Instead, she pounded the wood harder with her hammer.

The girl kept up the volume. "Well I'm crying because Mom said go outside 'cause I cried 'cause she wouldn't let me have Kitty Kat Krunchies for breakfast and I'm hungry."

"Oh." Catherine tried digging a hole with the heel of her boot.

"And Patrick told me to shut up and I think he hid my dolly and I can't find her and I have to go to pretty school again and I don't want to." The girl took in a big breath, and fresh tears sprang to her eyes.

"Pretty school?" Catherine straightened and frowned at the child. "Oh, preschool. If you're five, why aren't you in kindergarten?"

The girl pouted. "Mom says I couldn't get into kindergarten, because she made us leave Dad and it was the end of summer and we didn't tell them we were coming." The girl had choked out the words, adding extra whimpers for effect.

Catherine pursed her lips. "What is your name?"

"Tazzy," came the tearless answer, her eyes suddenly bright.

"That's not a name. What's your real name?" She didn't mean to sound so harsh.

"It *is* my name. I gave it to me 'cause Mom says I'm always hungry like the Tasmanian Devil, and I am, so you can call me Tazzy for short."

Catherine smiled. "Well, Miss Tazzy, I hope you don't eat these tomato stakes for breakfast if you're that hungry." She twisted the pointed end of the stake, trying to make a dent in the ground.

The child scrunched her face, eyeing Catherine's progress. "I don't like tomatoes or steaks, but I do like cereal and graham crackers—do you have any?"

Catherine lowered her knees and gouged the dirt with the claw end of the hammer. "No, I don't think so." She sat back on her ankles and softened her voice but avoided looking at the girl, now at eye level. "But I guess your mom will make you something good for breakfast."

Tazzy dragged her toe through the mud in front of Catherine's stake. "No, she won't. She just says she'll give me a smack if I ask for Kittie Kat Krunchies again, so I came out here to see what you're doing and to see your dog again—what's his name?"

Catherine dropped the hammer. It had done nothing but splinter the top of the stake and blister her finger; the solid earth refused to be moved.

She turned to Tazzy. "His name is Percy and he's five like you. But he's having a nap right now."

"Can I wake him up?" The girl had lowered the volume but raised the pitch. She came closer to Catherine, who still held the stake.

"No." Catherine stood and cleared her throat. "Not right now. Maybe later."

The tiny girl's arms became stiff as sticks. "He likes me, and he doesn't bite me." She hunched her shoulders and moved past Catherine toward the path.

"I said no." Catherine lunged a giant step backwards, blocking the girl.

The child's lower lip jutted out. She stared up at Catherine's forehead and pointed, her voice loud again. "Does it hurt? Where's your boo-boo sticker? I wanted to come back, but your big wooden door was shut, and anyway, Patrick said I couldn't."

Catherine relaxed and shifted her feet. "Oh, that's okay, see, I'm fine. All better." She slid her bangs aside to reveal the small scab. "Maybe you can come visit Percy tomorrow." What am I saying? she thought.

Tazzy stared with her lips slack. Closing her mouth and wiping her nose, she tilted her head at the gate behind Catherine. Seconds later, she twirled away, grabbed a stake from the dirt, and lifted it high like a sword. She charged across the yards, whooping and hollering. Her coat slid off of her shoulders and hung at her elbows. The crows scattered from where they had landed in the street. She circled the mailbox, then ran up her front steps, brandishing her weapon and glaring at Catherine. Without a word, she threw the wood to the ground and slammed back into the house, her bright red scarf waving from the bush that had snagged it.

Catherine's legs still straddled the walkway. She stared at her stakes where they lay on the ground, then glanced up at the neighbor's front door glass. Still twitching from the impact, the reflection showed clouds moving in, smothering the sun and muting the sky.

Such a volatile, emotional little thing.

Why doesn't the mother come looking for her daughter?

None of your concern. Mind your own business.

She seems sick a lot; her nose is always running. Maybe someone should call the authorities.

Catherine kicked a clod of grassy dirt, and gathered her unused stakes. "I'll work on my boundaries another day." She trudged back into her garage.

17. Padlock and Visitor

Catherine hadn't seen those renters in over a week. After her failed attempt at staking out her territory, she was a bit disappointed Tazzy had not come back to visit Percy. The days were so cold, people kept to themselves. They hurried from their cars to their homes and huddled under heavy blankets in front of their televisions. The boy's school bus rumbled out front every weekday morning and afternoon. She assumed the girl was in preschool most days. One afternoon, a van dropped her off in the driveway. Why wasn't Patty around to bring her home?

Catherine was trying not to mind the cold and isolation. She had Percy, her blankets and books, and an occasional sip of Southern Comfort to warm her. But sometimes she'd find herself frozen at the mailbox, envelopes in hand, staring down the road at the unfinished sidewalks and half-built homes.

She shuddered and continued her search for an old cookbook in the garage. Weaving through the stacks of plastic containers, she stumbled across that red toolbox again. Sidestepping the boxes marked MOTHER, she reached to lift its rusty lid. The padlock lay in the top tray, open and twisted in a question mark. She held its cool body in her hand, feeling its weight. Catherine rummaged in the depths of the box with her other hand but found no key. Only a few sharp pokes on her fingertips from the loose screws and nails.

Why bother with all these things you keep for later but can't recall when you need them?

Better here than in a trash heap. You never know what you missed until you find it.

Catherine dangled the lock like a dead mouse. She marched out of the garage and around the side of the house. Standing inside her open gate, she looped the padlock around the metal staple without fastening the hasp. She'd have to find the missing key soon to keep that Tasmanian Devil from tearing up her yard.

"I came back to see your dog. Is he sleeping?"

Catherine startled and turned to the girl standing on her path, puffy pink coat zipped up to her chin, arms sticking out stiffly from her sides. Thick mud clung to the bottom and edges of her sneakers, as if she'd just slogged through a bog.

"Have you been in the creek, Tazzy?"

"No, Mom says don't go in the creek." She answered Catherine in a quick monotone, her mouth muffled by her scarf and her nose sounding stuffed up.

"Where'd you get all that mud then?"

Tazzy dropped her eyes to her feet for two seconds then lifted her chin. "I don't know!"

Catherine smiled at the child's stiff little body and sincere frown. She glanced across the lawn. No sign of the mother.

"You know, the creek can get high and dangerous after it rains. You could get stuck or fall in, so obey your mother and stay away from it. You have to be careful." Catherine pressed the gate open another inch, looking past the girl to her house.

The girl twisted her torso back toward her driveway. No sign of the brother or mother.

She swung toward Catherine again. "Okay, I'll be careful—can I see Percy?" The child marched forward, then wiggled through the gap in the gate to stand at attention in front of Catherine.

Catherine laid her hand on top of Tazzy's head and sighed. "Sure. But just for a minute." She stepped back, examining the child's feet. "And you'll have to take your muddy shoes off before going inside. Tazzy—"

The girl ran past her to the patio, kicked off her sneakers, and peeled away her socks. She flew up the steps, flung the door open, and rushed into Catherine's kitchen. "Percy, Percy, puppy dog, I'm here, I'm here," she sang.

Catherine followed her into the house. The coat was already on the floor, and her hands were all over the dog who'd come wagging into her arms. While Percy licked her cheeks, the room grabbed the girl's attention. She marveled at the kitchen's soft yellow walls and brightly patterned plates on open shelves.

"It's like the kitchens in Mom's magdazines."

"Magazines," Catherine corrected. She followed Tazzy as she ran to admire the daisies in a vase on the table before running her hand along a clean, uncluttered counter. "I'm in a store at the mall." She plopped her bare feet along the cool hardwood floor and trailed her fingers on the white cabinet doors. She stopped short at the tall pantry and yanked it open.

Catherine hurried to intervene. The girl investigated every shelf as if it held hidden treasures. "Don't open my cabinets without asking, young lady."

Tazzy grabbed a box of sugary cereal, Catherine's guilty pleasure, and flopped to the floor, diving in with a grimy hand. Percy closed in on the scene like a shark to blood, slathering the little girl with his tongue as she ate and giggled.

Catherine shut the cabinet door with her shoulder, reminding herself to wipe it down later. She leaned to watch the crime in progress on her kitchen floor.

She acts like she's starving. And she has a cold.

Better get her out of here before she spreads her germs everywhere. And before the mother gets wind of you letting her in here.

After allowing her to eat for a minute, Catherine picked up the coat and said, "Tazzy, time to go home. I'm sure your mother wonders where you are."

Tazzy stood, dangling the box by its green flap, her eyebrows arched.

"Yes, take it." Catherine shook her head and smiled. She ushered the girl out the back door and helped her get her socks and muddy shoes back on her feet. They found Patrick motionless on his porch steps, looking miserable and scared. His chest dropped in relief when he saw his sister coming toward him across the lawns.

"Tazzy, Mom's gonna kill you! What are you doing? Come back inside before she gets home. Hurry!"

He lifted his hand for a quick wave but kept his eyes lowered, never noticing Catherine's smile. The girl marched up the steps and past him into the house, waving the box of cereal like a captured flag. The door slammed.

Those poor children. They don't have a chance with a mother like that.

You don't know what the mother is like, really.

Catherine cleared her throat. "Oh, I know exactly what that mother is like."

She pulled her gate shut and settled her frame against it, taking in her haven, her domain. The cold season had certainly dulled its impact. She thought she'd be more excited about having finished the yard even though its completion coincided with the coming of winter.

That little devil has got you all stirred up.

She does have a lot of life in her.

She'll tear up more than your yard.

Shivering, Catherine looked for signs of life down by the creek. The willow tree waved her bare arms, sending a muted message. She was tall and strong yet also an aging tree that couldn't live forever.

What did you expect? A fairy godmother to zap your backyard garden into an ageless paradise?

Too bad no magic happens inside this fence, Miss Catherine. Fantasyland. Time for a reality check.

No harm in wishing upon a star.

Praying for a miracle, Old Woman?'

Catherine shook her head. "Would settle for an early spring, thank you."

18. Miss Laffer

The steely sky gave up the last of its light to a few weak streetlamps. Catherine was a shadow at her kitchen window watching Patty scrape ice from her windshield. She was using a child's plastic shovel and had shimmied herself onto the hood to reach the middle, thrashing and slipping in her soaked coat.

Probably going to a bar to meet up with some other losers. Leaving kids home alone is a crime.

She's always gone, and her yard is a mess—just like her hair. Things cannot be right over there.

Look who's talking. That head of yours is a cuckoo's nest. Not hurting anyone, though. Like some people we know.

Patty stomped back into her house, leaving the car running. Catherine thought of Miss Laffer and wondered what happened to her.

Her fourth-grade teacher, Miss Laffer, looked a lot like this woman, although she was far prettier and much more approachable. Probably dead by now.

Miss Laffer was a plump twenty-something, but she moved with energy and confidence. Her nylon stockings rubbed against her bright polyester dresses as she swished around the classroom. Young Catherine inhaled her flowery perfume and caressed her sleek fingernail polish whenever the teacher leaned in to help with a worksheet or correct a mistake. Always kind and calm, the smiling young woman drew quiet Catherine out of her shell. Lingering after class to help with erasers and papers, Catherine imbibed Miss Laffer's love of learning. She planted the seeds for Catherine's dream of becoming a teacher herself one day.

It was also Miss Laffer who asked her about the red marks on her arm and face.

Of course, Catherine always lied.

Miss Laffer might say, "Did you fall, Catherine? Your cheek looks a little bruised."

She would answer without hesitation. "No, I bumped into the school bus door before it was the whole way open. The driver felt so bad." She touched her face and shook her head.

Once when the indentations on her arm had browned to scabs, Miss Laffer examined her skin with her pretty fingers. "What happened here, Catherine? Looks like a wild animal got hold of you."

"Oh, that's funny because my friend's new puppy actually did bite me while we were playing. It looks worse than it is." She even pictured the imaginary pup as she told the tale.

Catherine was tempted to tell the truth. But Mother preempted the questions with threats. And anyway, young Catherine felt rather clever when the stories she told came marching from her lips without missing a beat. Her explanations of falling from trees, tripping on steps, or slipping in the creek seemed to satisfy her teacher.

"You're so accident prone, Catherine. Do you think you need glasses?"

Now that she thought of it, squinting to watch Patty's car slide out of her driveway and spin down the hill, Catherine wondered why her favorite teacher had never suspected her of lying. Or did she?

Perhaps Miss Laffer had decided the signs were not clear enough, not worth further investigation. Catherine sighed and closed her eyes, picturing the marks on Tazzy's arm, the worry on Patrick's face, the neglect that showed on both of those kids. She let the curtain fall back across the darkened window. Indeed, she needed to do a little investigating.

19. Spilling Over

Catherine turned up the burner and stirred her homemade chicken soup. The high heat brought the edges of the broth close to boiling, and when she shut off the gas, a rush of steam escaped as if in relief.

"C'mon, Percy, let's eat lunch in the front room." She poured her soup and grabbed a pack of crackers from the pantry. She liked to think of her sitting room as a kind of old- fashioned parlor, her best furniture arranged for admiring her collection of botanical prints. She placed her food on the metal tray table by the front window and noticed the neighbor kids jostling each other on the sidewalk.

Catherine leaned to unlock and lift the window. Her head against the screen but unseen, she listened in on the argument.

"I need some space." Tazzy shouldered Patrick's hand away.

Patrick grabbed her arm. "You can't go over there. It's not safe by that empty house. And anyway, Mom says we're not supposed to cross the road." He was shouting.

"Where is Mom?" Tazzy flung her arm out to release his grip, her lips turning downward.

His voice was edged with tears. "Mom will be home soon. She's working."

The little girl's hair was a matted mess, and both kids were without coats. The mother, Patty, was nowhere in sight. Catherine could swear her car hadn't been in the driveway for a few days.

Patrick now dragged his sister by the arm. She broke away from him and fell on her hands. Howling with rage and frustration, she darted across the street.

"Mom will kill you if she finds out you went over there," he called across to her.

"I don't get why you have to boss me around. You're not the parent!" Her face was crumpled, her cheeks streaked with tears.

The boy squared his shoulders with arms on hips. "Mom said I am in charge when she's not here and you have to listen to me." He looked down the road, his voice now pleading. "Come over here, Tazzy, please. You can have your space. Just stay in our yard."

Tazzy stepped off the curb towards Patrick just as a car crested the hill. It was going too fast.

Catherine jumped up, scalding her thigh with her soup. She ran to open her front door. Before she could get the outer door unlocked, she saw that the car had slowed, the driver aware of the child in the road. Catherine exhaled a groan, surprising herself with the sound. Even Percy turned from licking up the spill.

The girl finished crossing. She ran past her brother, hitting him hard in his stomach as she went.

The poor boy followed his little sister back to their yard. Tazzy had skipped up their steps and was now spinning at the top. She stopped to stick out her tongue, then suck it back in like a spaghetti noodle. Next, she opened her arms wide, lifted her chin to the sky, and let out her favorite bratty scream.

20. Patrick

Patrick dragged the empty trash can back from the curb, his sandy-blond bangs swinging in his eyes. After settling the big plastic container in its place on the side of the house, he plopped down on the front stoop and picked up a notebook. His lips moved as he read. He didn't see Catherine approach.

With a stiff wave, she called across the driveway. "Hello there, Patrick!"

"Oh, hi, Miss Hathaway, how are you today?" He stood and strolled toward her, smiling.

She smiled back and took a few more steps in his direction. "I'm doing well, thank you. I haven't seen you in quite some time. How is your school year going?"

They met where their yards adjoined. Looking up at her, he shrugged and stayed silent, considering her question. After a few seconds, he said, "It's been fine. School is hard this year, but I'm learning a lot and I really like fifth-grade science." His countenance was relaxed, his speech methodical.

"I'm glad to hear that. Did you know I was a fifth-grade teacher for many years? I loved teaching science and writing." She had unfolded her arms, attempting to hold them open and relaxed at her side.

"No, I didn't know that." He seemed genuinely interested, his freckled cheeks lifting as he spoke. "I like science, but I *love* writing. In fact, I'm working on a novel." He lifted his notebook but lowered his eyes. "I'm afraid it's not very good. Has a few holes in the plot. Maybe you could help me with it?" He wrinkled his nose and looked up at her from under his bangs.

"I would be glad to help. Tell me what the story is about?" Catherine's hands were clasped behind her, she swayed side to side as if listening to a student in her classroom.

"Okay, sure. It's about a kid who has special powers . . ." He described how his hero, Jesse Warrant, fights to save the planet and his family from inside a video game. Jesse has amazing skills within the virtual world but believes he's helpless in real life.

He said, "Jesse beats the bad guys when they battle inside the game. But the evil forces are starting to break the rules and make incursions into the real world." His face tilted up, his blue eyes reflecting the sky. "The video game feeds Jesse's power but is luring him from his family, trying to trick him." Patrick frowned. "Sklar, the super villain, plans to land right in his yard and destroy his home when Jesse's lost in the game. He knows he's weak in the real world." He dropped his chin back to earth. "What do you think,

Miss Hathaway? Does it sound like a story anyone would want to read?"

A woodpecker punctuated the pause but could not compete for Catherine's attention. She rocked on her heels in the grass. Her eyes traced the branches of the maple above, but she saw only the boy's tale playing out in her head.

"Yes." Her gaze stayed high. "I think it's wonderful. You have elements of suspense, character motivation, and symbolism. Jesse's goal and the lie he believes create his conflict, which is a specific and yet universal theme." She lowered her chin and beamed at him. "I believe you will find a way to fill any plot holes by letting Jesse become who he needs to be." The look on Patrick's face told her that she had dumped a load of groceries when all he wanted was a cookie.

Catherine laughed, the delicate skin around her eyes crinkling. "Sorry, Patrick, I got a bit excited. How about you tell me where you're stuck in the story?"

He smiled and hugged the notebook. "Well, Jesse wants to save the world, defeat that evil Sklar. But he—I—can't figure out how to keep his family safe at the end, when he's lost in the game." He stared straight ahead, his expression connecting to the dilemma. He looked up at Catherine again. "Do you think he needs a secret weapon?"

"Maybe Jesse needs another character, a mentor. You know, like Yoda in Star Wars or Harry's Dumbledore. Somebody to help Jesse find his hidden strength."

He thought it over, head tilted. His face seemed suddenly hot. His eyes widened. "I think what I'm missing is a force field. Jesse can create an invisible wall around himself and become impenetrable, completely closed off behind his shield. Maybe his secret weapon is using this force field whenever he and his family are being attacked."

Catherine's heart pounded in her throat. A mother wren trilled her song, her whole body engaged as she perched upon the gate. A chorus of wren-song followed, her brood responding like chimes in the wind. Catherine and the boy stood silent, each swirling in their own thoughts, their feet on the line where the stakes were supposed to be.

Catherine began. "Patrick, do you . . . does your . . ." The change in her tone brought his eyes to hers. She continued. "I was just wondering if you need help with, well, more than your story about Jesse. Is there anything that's happening at your house that makes you scared?"

Catherine feared she had gone too far, gotten too specific. Would the boy even trust her with an honest answer about his mother?

Patrick tilted his head and frowned up at her for several seconds, his hair falling too long onto one shoulder. "I'm not . . . I don't think so." He was wary, suddenly shut down. Catherine averted her eyes, noted the holes in the knees of his jeans.

She pressed on despite the backward tug in her mind. "Sometimes I see marks on Tazzy. And you look anxious to me."

Patrick crinkled his eyebrows, then smiled. "Oh—oh, yeah, well, Tazzy falls down a lot from all of her spinning and running around." He rolled his eyes. "And, she spilled hot chocolate on her leg the other day. Mom was gone and said I was in charge. The man of the house now. I didn't really know what to do, so I made her get in the shower with cold water in case she had a burn."

Catherine kept at it. "Now, does your mother come home every night? I hope you're not left alone for—"

"Yeah, she works a lot and works late sometimes but . . ." He stopped, his face a mask. "Mom says to keep our business to ourselves, and I guess she wouldn't want me talking about all this stuff." He shuffled his feet and they both stared at the space between them.

Catherine inhaled sharply through her nose, drawing her lips into a thin line and clipping her words. "All right, I understand. I'm sorry. I know it's none of my business." Her cheeks were burning. "But if you ever need anything or want me to help with your story, just let me know." She tried to sound cheerful, lighthearted, attaching a smile to her face.

The boy matched her voice and smiled up at her. "Thanks, Miss Hathaway, I'll do that." He slid the notebook under his arm and pounced up the steps. He slipped into the house but gave her a quick wave, catching the door just before it slammed.

21. Under the Skin

Catherine had forgotten to plant new tulip bulbs before the cold set in. She'd regret it in a few weeks when the world showed signs of life but no tulips poked their heads above ground. Without the promise of those early risers, she had fewer reasons for getting out of her own bed. When winter dragged its feet and spring refused to pick up the pace, her energy flagged with them.

From her recliner beside the window, Percy napping on her lap, Catherine took in her view of the backyard. Not much happening out there, just a wash of grayish beige. Leaf litter from those old oaks, which she'd left as a plant cover, muted most of her evergreens and red twig dogwoods. Even the flashing scarlet cardinals were dulled in their jackets. She scoured the ground. Had her year-round robins taken a vacation from her winter haven?

Catherine pulled Mother's heavy old quilt close around her shoulders, scowling at the scars in the yard where a mole had plowed its paths. Its upraised tunnels mounded through one side of her lawn and into the tulip patch.

Last fall, the invisible vermin had disrupted the entire bed where dozens of bulbs nestled in the loamy earth it loved so much. She had stomped with heavy boots along each line of the mole's grub mine, a temporary collapse of its dirty work. Hours later, when she went to tuck her bulbs back to sleep, she discovered an empty bed. Chipmunks and squirrels must've stolen most of her precious tulips. Now months later, the mole had created a fresh mountain range. She seethed at his impertinence and tenacity, judging the innocent creature with criminal intent. Of course, he could not see the effect of his disrespect. Nonetheless, she must get rid of the disruptive little thing.

Staring through the icy window, Catherine whispered, "It's the little things that get under your skin." Like tiny hidden tunnels, the doubt, regret, resentment, and lies can undermine the entire structure of a life.

Falling down from spinning and running around.

Really? That's how Patrick had explained the marks on his sister's skin. What if it was just a cover-up? Clever lies his mother forced him to tell. He *was* becoming a fiction writer. Was there a real Sklar in his life? A frightening force he feared? Perhaps a selfish parent who couldn't see the damage she was doing.

A soft growl rumbled in Percy's throat, his legs quivering from a doggy-dream chase. Catherine smiled and rested a hand on his side, careful not to wake him.

Maybe he could earn his keep this spring by ferreting out moles with those sharp claws. He was a terrier, after all.

The birthmark on her forearm drew her eye. She traced it with her left forefinger, outlining the large brown oval painted above her wrist. It was faded and smaller than when she was young. Mother called it her pretty spot whenever she complained that kids teased her about it.

"Can I have it taken off?"

"Stop being silly. It's your birthmark—it proves you're alive."

"But it's so big. And so dark. Everybody can see it. They think it's weird."

"Who cares what they think. Just worry about yourself."

"But what if they think *I'm* weird?"

"You can't have it both ways, Catherine Hathaway: you're either taking care of yourself or you're taking care of someone else."

Mother was good at taking care of herself. At least for a short time. In the long run, drinking and sleeping around ended with the kind of problems one must take care of or they'd take care of you. Like Baby June. And alcoholism.

Catherine didn't know about alcoholic hepatitis until a homeless shelter in Portland had written her a letter and sent a few personal papers. According to the shelter, Mother didn't know herself by the time she died. But she did keep track of her daughter. Catherine's name and address were with her few belongings. Mother never contacted her in her final years. The shelter workers had cared for her knowing nothing of her past.

Carla Hathaway was just forty-years-old when she disappeared from that hole-in-the-wall apartment, leaving those boxes and no forwarding address for Catherine. Nine years later, Mother was dead. Gone from Catherine's life forever.

The light shifted. The world tilted further from the sun. Catherine touched the cold pane, the quilt slipping from her shoulders. Since she'd retired, trickles of distant memories seeped through cracks in her tightly sealed walls. They wound their way along rutted surfaces that hadn't been touched in decades. It went against her grain to let memories get the best of her. She let the past be the past. But that was an old habit that was asking for change.

Let sleeping dogs lie.

That's what Mother had always said when, as a girl, Catherine asked questions about her father or about Mother's childhood. Dad was a blank page Catherine filled with her imagination. Mother, a closed window, locked and painted shut.

She did remember a black and white photo of her parents from before she was born, the kind with the white scalloped edges lending importance to the moment. Where did it end up? she wondered. Her smiling father with a cigarette in his mouth, a guitar resting on one knee, her beautiful young mother on the other—both looked so happy in the photo, so unencumbered.

Mother spoke once of how Catherine's father wasted his time reading books and writing poetry. The final bitter story sketched a dad with a drug addiction that had led to his tragic death from overdose. Mother and Father had never married. He only knew his baby girl for a few months before he passed away. Mother had never forgiven him for leaving her with a kid to raise. She never forgave herself for anything, either. She heard her Mother's words:

Catherine Hathaway, you only get what you deserve.

Touching her birthmark again, Catherine wondered what she deserved. Mother never forgave her for keeping the card the CPS lady slipped into her hand that day. Had Catherine forgiven Mother for the pain she'd left in her crushing wake? The ladies weighed in.

Doesn't matter that you weren't there for her when she died. She never was for you.

Still, if you had searched, you may have found her before it was too late.

Too late for what, Old Woman? You couldn't save her. Or save anybody else for that matter. You'll be glad when your time at the trough is up.

Go on and live to one hundred years old, Miss Catherine. Just keep to yourself. It goes better that way.

It's true, thought Catherine. No one needs me. I could choose to be done with it. Or make a case for carrying on.

She stroked Percy's head and wondered if the ladies would ever go away, leave her in peace. Would they be satisfied if she ignored every closeted skeleton? Or dredged up and spilled every last drop of her history like a bucket on the bare brown earth?

Don't go digging in that wishing well, Old Woman. You'll drown with no one to save you.

Forget the past. Maybe the best is yet to come.

That's magical thinking. At seventy, nothing gets better. It's all downhill from here.

Magical things can happen inside high fences.

Nah. You only get what you deserve.

Catherine stood and slid Percy to the cushion, hoping he'd stay asleep. Instead, his eyes shot open, his ears perked up, his body braced for their next adventure. She cupped his chin in her palm.

"Percy, it's time to make that phone call. When I was a kid, a neighbor cared enough to make the call for me."

He wagged his tail, jumped from the chair, and followed her to where the telephone waited on the wall.

Spring

"Is the spring coming?" he said. "What is it like? ..."

"It is the sun shining on the rain and the rain falling on the sunshine, and things pushing up and working under the earth ..."

—Frances Hodgson Burnett, *The Secret Garden*

"Perhaps," she said, leaning forward a little, "you will tell me your name. If we are to be friends"—she smiled her grave smile—"as I hope we are, we had better begin at the beginning."

—Elizabeth von Armin, *The Enchanted April*

22. Robins and Mud Puddles

Spring was Catherine's favorite season. When it stepped into the picture, there was no going back. Sure, the cold loitered in the mornings, but it moved along when the sun burst on the scene. A few satisfying rays by midday and even the morning frost couldn't convince the world that the cold would last forever. Winter had closed the lid on itself, and spring was slowly opening its treasure chests of colorful gems.

Catherine inspected her azaleas for early buds. She was getting ahead of herself. Let the flowers unfold on their own, she chuckled, remembering an old rhyme:

> *I hurried the lily and bid her to bloom*
> *To show us her beauty, her beauty to prove*
> *I hurried the lily and missed what she was*
> *Becoming perfection and lovely enough*

Beauty will arrive precisely when you're not looking for it, she reminded herself, turning toward the creek with a smile. The willow was waking from her winter nap. Her lithe limbs waved in the warming air, pale branches reaching for the greening bank.

Catherine tucked her hands into her folded arms. She had not made the call to CPS after all. The fear of making a mistake kept her from taking many actions. The last thing she wanted was to add to her list of failed attempts at doing the right thing.

What to do, what to do? played over and over like a broken record in her head.

The song refused to resolve itself and let her think. Nevertheless, she mustn't jump to conclusions; better to give the mother, Patty, some small benefit of her many doubts.

The afternoon was winding down, early evening close on its heels. But Catherine felt fresh in her green gauzy skirt topped with a white button-up blouse. The invisible fingers of a breeze lifted her hair from her neck and ruffled the cotton fabric along her skin. She was put together for a change. Watering her potted succulents, she watched a robin weave crazy cadences across the lawn.

She admired the robin's maneuvers. First, a headlong rush with hunched body forward, committed to the march. Then, a sudden stop, legs taut, body up, head tilted toward the ground. Catherine called it the dash-dash-statue dance. Not easily frightened to flight like the mourning dove, the robin was a solid ground bird. Always out scouting, never near the feeders, the robin alternated between making an effort and pausing for perspective.

If a bird I were to be, a common robin would be me.

Catherine hummed a rhyme she'd created. Unremarkable but steady and resilient, she was a four-seasons kind of old bird, dashing for survival then pausing to check her surroundings. Unfortunately, her tippy-toes didn't always give her the view she wanted. The expanse of the path often froze her like a stone, poised to roll back or stumble forward. Nevertheless, she kept on like the robin: work then pause to regroup. Headlong rush to the task at hand, stop for reassessment.

Catherine propped her watering can beneath the rain barrel and twisted the spigot. Her shoulder rested against the brick wall as the water filled the metal container. With her feet bare to the cool earth, she was less a dashing robin lately and more of a stone statue.

She tilted her head at the sounds of the working world about her. The air conditioner hummed on the side of the house. A lawnmower roared a few yards over. Somewhere close by, a worker blasted his radio. His music and cigarette smoke rode the wind up and over Catherine's fence. The Eagles sang, "Peaceful, Easy Feeling" and she joined the chorus: *I know you won't let me down. Cause I'm already standin' on the ground.*

She didn't mind the sounds of life surrounding her sanctuary, the work in progress. Like the birds, she took responsibility for her own happiness. She found out a long time ago that for everything to be all right she had to be all right with everything. Catherine sighed, poking at a hole between bricks where the mortar had crumbled. *Knowing how to be* didn't necessarily translate into *being how you wanted.* Peaceful didn't always come easy.

Unless you were a dog. Percy was a perfect example of accepting life as it is. And living it to the fullest. From Percy's perspective, every inch of the garden's wet grass had a tale to tattle, every low leaf a crime to report, all of which he was determined to detect.

This morning as soon as she'd opened the back door, he catapulted himself down the steps and across the lawn. His wiry head bobbled, tethered to a nose with a mind of its own. Where the roving snout directed, the stout brown body followed. Catherine loved to watch him rush around the yard, imagining what his simple life was like.

The little terrier ping-ponged inside the borders of his domain, inhaling every molecule of evidence, each clue to last night's intruders, before pausing to pee. In this patch of grass, he probably smelled a coyote who'd rumbled through. And yes, over there it had stopped to sniff the compost heap before slinking across the creek. Oh, and between those bushes, an owl surprised a skunk, which left a heavy dose of itself on the roses. Aha, that nasty orange cat dared to squat in the fresh mulch beneath the hydrangea. Was she still lurking beside the woodpile where the chipmunks lived?

He propelled himself past the pile of logs, chasing mama rabbit back under the fence to the neighbor's taller grass. Pausing on the edge of the creek bordering his woods, the little dog inhaled deeply, lifting his black crusty nose in sweeps to catch each draft. He knew somewhere far under those trees deer foraged. They couldn't hide their musky stink from him.

To Catherine's dismay, Percy finished his rounds by starting a barking contest with the closest neighbor dogs, also out for their morning sniffs. Those mutts three houses down were always game for a solid thirty-second alarm. How else would all of their people know the dogs were on the job?

This morning when Catherine called him back to the house, Percy practiced his art of delayed obedience. First he lifted his leg on his favorite dogwood. Then he dashed toward the usual squirrels, stopping short of bothering with them. Although they waited for him to start the chase, he knew he couldn't catch them now. Those fluff-tailed rodents scaled the big wooden wall in a flash; their squeezing squeals of indignation were just for show. As was his barking from the ground below.

But ever so slowly, as always, he made his way back to her.

Catherine reckoned Percy didn't mind the new fence. It helped him avoid those guilty moments returning from a chase that had taken him far into neighboring yards. He knew his boundaries. He always returned penitent, finding her with arms on hips in confirmation of his shame. Yes, before the wall and gate arrived, asking permission to chase a trespassing possum or follow his nose toward the road never occurred to him. Asking forgiveness was his specialty.

Percy learned early in his life with Catherine that forgiveness was a given and patience paid off. He lived for their walks. An instinct deep in his brain made him stop on the edge of the bridge to the woods until she slid into her walking shoes and lifted that hickory stick. "Now we're going places."

Yesterday morning had been different.

A heavy rain had soaked the world the night before, stirring up plants and animals alike. Catherine's sinuses were stirred up, too. And her joints flared with the change in barometric pressure. A dizzy spell sent her back to bed after she opened the back door to let Percy out. Not that lying down helped. The ceiling spun until she shut her eyes. But then the universe swirled in the blackness. After the worst passed, she grunted upright again, using her hands to settle each leg on the floor. Percy had probably waited for her for fifteen minutes beside the hum of the running water. Maybe he scratched an ear and stared at the back door. But her timing was off. The signals were mixed. His routine was shaken.

Once she remembered Percy was outside alone, Catherine thrust her head and torso forward, letting the momentum bring her to her feet. Like Frankenstein's monster, she wobbled from her bedroom, through the living room, and into the kitchen, where she tottered out the back door. He wasn't waiting for her at the edge of the creek by the log bridge. She whistled. Whistled again—this time with two fingers in her mouth, shrill, and loud as she could, signaling her annoyance with a ping of fear.

"Percy. Percy, get over here." Her hands formed a megaphone. "Come."

The school bus rumbled and squealed in the distance, making its way around the neighborhood, coming closer to where it stopped for Patrick. The creek was louder than usual and had risen considerably from the rain. She whistled again, then shouted in her loudest, most-piercing tone. Still, the dog didn't show.

Catherine fumbled for her walking stick, nearly knocking it down the steps from where it leaned on the railing. She caught the polished branch in one hand and the rail in the other, negotiating the short flight as if it was a cliff. At the bottom, she called again. "Percy! Hey!" The fear was thick in her throat. "Come back."

No sign of the mutt. She took a deep breath then let out a high-pitched, "Treat! Treat!"

The school bus throttled along the road, going too fast. Drawn by the commotion, she discovered her gate sat half open. Catherine's knees buckled. The downshifting gears and screeching brakes announced its last stop in front of the neighbors' house.

"No." Blood thumped in her ears. "Not the front, never the front."

She reached her drive just as the bus stopped for Patrick. He raced out of his house, shirt flying up around his belly and backpack hanging off an elbow. The front lawns were empty. Nothing under the bus wheels. No sign of the dog.

"Patrick, Patrick, have you seen my little dog, Percy?" she shouted, forgetting her swirling head and unkempt hair.

He whirled at the bottom step of the bus. "What? Oh, no, Miss Hathaway, I haven't. I'm sorry. I gotta go."

The door hissed shut, and the bus sputtered off. Catherine turned a circle, semi-conscious of nausea, in awe of her body's extreme reaction.

"Miss Hathaway, have you seen Tazzy?"

Catherine wheeled to face Patty leaning out her front door. Her short robe sagged open, her hair drooped half-curled, and a makeup brush hung in her hand.

Catherine's brain drew a blank, but it managed to stir up some words. "Uh, Tazzy? No, I was looking for my dog."

They moved toward each other, both spinning and scanning in all directions.

"I get so mad when she just goes off without telling me . . ." Patty's eyes avoided Catherine's.

"Percy never goes anywhere without me." The road was crawling with cars.

"Tazzy, Taahhzzy!" Patty's voice was strangled.

"Percy, treat, Perrrrcy!" Catherine tried not to shriek.

They stopped shouting and stood listening. A sound rose above the rushing creek and the rumbling rush hour out on the highway.

The women spun toward the bank at the back of Patty's yard. They heard it again. A cry, a bark, a scream?

Patty flew through the grass with Catherine close behind, digging her stick into the earth to keep pace.

It was a perilous journey through the slick grass. After they had gone a few yards, Percy's bark rang out to their right.

The women slowed, turning their heads in unison. In a huge puddle on the far side of Patty's lawn sat Tazzy. Percy dashed along its edge, splashed by the girl. They were both covered in muck and buoyed with the joy of spring.

The women hurried to the scene.

"Peyton, get your butt up right now." Patty's voice sliced the air.

Catherine found her own cutting tone. "You could have killed Percy. He doesn't know about the road. Don't you ever open my gate again." Her shout pierced the peaceful scene. "Percy, come here, right now."

The guilty little creatures stared up at the women with shocked innocence. The dog ducked his head and tail to make himself smaller while the girl lifted a turtle high above her head.

"Mom, look at this! Look what I found in the grass!"

Patty turned to Catherine, her jaw tight. "Who cares about your dumb dog? At least you don't have to get him ready for school in five minutes." She turned back to the mud puddle. "Put that thing down and do what I told you to do. You have school today. You can't miss again."

The girl placed the turtle carefully in the swamp and stood. Slipping and sliding, she came toward them, her face an earthy smear and her hands pure clumps of mud.

Patty, with her half-curled, pink-tipped hair, stepped back from her daughter just as Catherine stepped in. She grabbed Tazzy's slimy hands as she skidded to a stop, nearly falling.

Tazzy jerked her hands from Catherine's.

"I didn't go through your stupid gate. Percy came around the fence by the creek to see me." The girl lifted her smudged chin to Catherine, then trudged past her and her mother. She slouched toward the house, her clothes clinging to her skin with an opaque brown sheen.

Patty followed. "Girl, don't you throw that attitude. Didn't I say to stay in the house while I was getting ready? You've got to start obeying. I don't want to have to smack you where the sun don't shine." She stabbed the air with her finger. The little girl slid her hands to her backside, running faster toward their door.

Catherine watched them go, her mind jumbled, her stomach fluttering. It wasn't the girl's fault Percy had gone around the fence. It was her own fault. She couldn't blame Percy for growing impatient and following his instincts. She had stayed inside too long. She had left the gate open. She was the one to blame. She deserved to lose Percy—wouldn't it serve her right for being such a dolt?

But she didn't lose him. Her dog was safe and sound. And the girl, too.

Catherine wanted to call out to Patty and Tazzy, end the morning's story better than this. But the words wouldn't journey from her head to her lips. Her muddy hands stayed planted on her hips. Patty and Tazzy disappeared through the back door.

Percy sniffed his way farther from her. She whistled. He immediately circled back, tail high and tongue wagging. Muddy and triumphant he bounded to her side.

Love how he forgets to feel guilty for more than a minute.

Could use some of that amnesia juice.

Call it a forgive-and-forget tonic.

How about a love-and-mercy cocktail?

23. Nicknames and Snacks

But that was yesterday. Today was another story. A robin plucked a worm from the earth. Catherine had been holding her breath. She emptied her lungs in a rush and pressed a hand to her chest. Her white blouse was damp, limp on her skin. The peaceful, easy feeling had fled. The late afternoon sun slanted to a glare, and she wondered what to do about the kids next door. Lock the gate? Call the authorities? Bake some cookies?

She shut off the spigot, lifted the overflowing can, and walked lopsided to the patio. A small voice disrupted the settling dusk. She paused to listen. A child was crying.

Catherine turned, losing her grip on the watering can. It dropped, toppled sideways, and sent a tidal wave across the stone patio.

There it was again, close.

Catherine narrowed her eyes in the orange light. The little girl, Tazzy, hovered just inside the open gate with red cheeks and puffy eyes.

Heat flared in Catherine's chest. She must remind the girl about privacy and knocking. She hurried across the patio. The girl stood with fists at her side, gulping back sobs like huge hiccups.

"What's wrong, Tazzy?" The sky had mellowed to a cotton-candy pink and glowed on the girl's face, melting away Catherine's anger.

"Nothing. I'm just coming to see your flowers and Percy." She moved toward Catherine.

"Well, come over here and sit a minute."

Catherine lowered her ungainly frame onto the grass near the roses. She patted the spot beside her. Tazzy reached her in a few skipping hops and plopped down. She squinted up at Catherine.

"Hey, what're you doing out here in the dark?" Her voice had cleared, as if she'd forgotten the storm that had brought her through Catherine's gate.

"It's not dark yet. There's still a little light left." She pointed at the cottony clouds. Tazzy nodded and waved at the sky.

Catherine continued. "Do you know, little lady, that it's not polite to say *hey*? You can call me by my name."

"What's your name?"

"Miss Hathaway."

"No, your whole name."

"Catherine Hathaway."

"Do you have a nickname?"

"Well . . ." Catherine paused, watching the girl's crisscrossed legs bouncing on the grass. "Yes, I guess I do. But I don't use it."

"Why not?" The girl stretched her bare legs out straight and wiggled, her hands petting the thick grass beside her.

"It doesn't fit me, really. Stands out and calls attention to itself. My father gave it to me. Actually, no, *I* gave it to me."

"What is it?" The girl had stopped wriggling and was watching her with interest.

"Willow," she answered.

"Willow?" The girl spoke softly, twisting sideways to look at her. "Like the tree by the creek?" Her voice rose in a chirruping crescendo, reminding Catherine of the shy towhee's call.

She smiled down at the girl and rested her hand on the top of her head. "Yes, like my tree by the creek." They both turned to watch her branches dancing and hovering above the water. "How do you know it's a willow tree?"

The girl studied Catherine's face. "My mom told me. I like that name. I'm going to call you Willow." She jumped up and spun in a circle, her arms waving above her head.

Catherine leaned back to give the swinging arms wider berth. "I don't know—no one has ever called me that before."

"I do! Willow, Willow, Willow . . ." she sang.

Catherine stretched her arms behind her in the grass, leaning on her elbows and rearranging her hips on the ground. "I guess you can. I might forget it's me you're talking to if you call me Willow."

"I'll remind you. It'll be like *my* nickname: you can call me Tazzy Girl and I'll call you Willow Woman." The little girl paused mid-twirl, eyes wide. "Almost like Wonder Woman," she whispered. "Do you have any superpowers or invisible magic stuff?"

Catherine laughed. She shifted on the ground, sifting her new name through her old body. Invisible magic? She had hoped for some sort of enchantment, hadn't she?

Struggling upright to hug her knees, Catherine said, "Yes, I do, Tazzy Girl. I have two invisible lady friends who keep me company sometimes. And I have the power to talk to trees and other plants, and even animals. Sometimes I can hear what they're saying back to me." Her eyebrows lifted with her lips.

Tazzy froze, a grin growing beneath her rosy cheeks. "I told Patrick I saw you talking to the trees and Percy, and he didn't believe me!" She ran to hug Catherine sitting at eye-level in the grass. Catherine nearly tumbled sideways under the force. The girl let go, singing louder than ever, her arms flailing in the air. "Willow talks to the trees, Willow talks to the trees." She danced precariously close to the roses.

Catherine rolled to one knee and leaned hard on her other foot. She pushed herself to standing and moved toward the girl. Placing her hands lightly on her thin shoulders, she looked down.

"Don't fall on my flowers. They'll poke you with their thorns." The child's face lifted to hers. Catherine's heart turned soft and fuzzy. "Why were you crying when you came through the gate?"

Tazzy grew somber. "Well, I was just singing my songs and Patrick got mad and told me to be quiet 'cause he has to do his homework and Mom's in bed and he told me to play outside and I needa go to the bathroom and I'm sad."

Catherine touched the girl's cheek. "I'm sorry you're sad. What makes you happy?"

Tazzy's eyes slid around the yard. "I like birds and flowers and the creek. And Kitty Kat Krunchies."

"Do you like to go for walks?" Catherine thought of the paths that had soothed her own tears as a child.

"I don't know. I can't go for a walk by myself, because I have to stay in the yard. Do *you* like to go for walks?"

Catherine smiled, dropping her hands. "Yes, I do. I like to walk with Percy. Especially in those woods back there. It's better and safer than getting all muddy wading in the creek."

Tazzy looked up at her sideways, gauging her tone. "Can I go with you?"

Catherine shrugged and smiled. "Sure. We'll go on a Saturday morning sometime—but you'll have to ask your mom."

"She's sleeping and needs some space."

"Maybe when she's awake."

"Do you have any snacks, and can I go to the bathroom in your house?"

Catherine bit her lower lip and looked past her fence towards the girl's house. "Sure," she said. "Want some crackers and peanut butter?"

"Yeah and can I pet Percy?" Tazzy squirmed and danced.

Catherine lifted her empty watering can and set it upright on the stones.

Together, they headed toward the cool, dark house.

"I like to be in bare feet, too," Tazzy said, looking down at their toes. She slid her tiny hand into Catherine's.

Catherine switched on the kitchen light. Percy woke from his nap on her bed. Half of his face stayed folded in place as he darted through the living room and into the kitchen with a sleepy bark. He wagged his ecstatic body into the arms of the girl. Her red cheeks transformed with his licking.

"Here, give Percy a treat and he'll love you forever." Catherine handed the girl a cracker with a dab of peanut butter on it. Percy gobbled it in one snatch before Tazzy knew what was happening. "Now go in there to use the bathroom." She pointed toward the hallway. "And don't forget to wash your hands when you're finished."

Catherine put a plate of peanut butter crackers and a glass of milk on the table. She extended her hand when Tazzy reappeared a minute later.

"C'mon now, sit here and have a snack yourself. But don't let it ruin your supper." She pulled a chair out from under the table.

"Percy, I'll play with you in a minute." Tazzy skipped across the kitchen like a hungry little puppy.

Catherine watched the child eat. Legs swinging under the table, she gobbled the crackers and slurped her milk like it was the first food she'd had in a week.

When Tazzy finished, Catherine said, "It's getting late. Let's get you home so your mother doesn't worry. I'll walk you through the gate." She ushered the girl outside with a light squeeze on her sweaty little neck.

"I don't like your gate." Tazzy's voice was hushed.

"Why not?" Catherine stopped to look down at her.

"When it's shut it's too high for me to see if you and Percy are in the yard when I want to come over."

"I guess you'll have to knock and wait for me to say 'Who is it?'"

They descended the steps and rounded the corner. "What's that thing for?" The girl pointed to the open padlock dangling on the staple.

"That's my old padlock."

"What's it for?"

"To keep out the bad guys. And nosy little girls. But I haven't used it yet." She touched the tip of Tazzy's nose with a bony finger.

Tazzy hands jumped to her hips, her chin lifted, her eyes a challenge. "I can just climb around your fence by the creek like Percy does."

Catherine bent toward the girl. "Don't you dare do that. It's too deep and fast where the fence ends at the bank. Especially after it's rained. You could slip and fall in." She was kneeling now, locking her eyes on Tazzy's, gripping both her hands to accentuate the message.

Tazzy laughed, yanked her hands from Catherine's, and placed them on either side of Catherine's face. She squeezed, looking at Catherine through her sandy eyelashes.

"I can learn to swim. And someday I'll just come right up into your yard like a giant turtle and say, 'Hey, Willow Woman.'" Tazzy pressed their foreheads together. Two seconds later, she was running through the open gate, hooting and waving her arms. Catherine straightened and smiled. As she watched the girl go, her shoulders softened and settled, creating more space in the front of her chest.

24. Baby Bird

Unzipping her jacket, Catherine inhaled a sweet draft—the scent of spring: fervency mixed with melancholy. Her seasons were counting down, and her heart searched harder for its kindling. Every fresh breeze fanned what sparks remained. Every new leaf fed the energy within. Stiff as a scarecrow in her vegetable garden, she was grateful for the planting and tending, which kept her moving, made her strong, and gave her an appetite.

Catherine dragged a spade along the surface of the dirt, marking rows for spring lettuces and spinach. A commotion arose in a nearby oak. Several robins chirped in alarm from their low branches. Catherine planted the shovel and scanned the grass below their clamor. Sure enough, a baby bird. Probably toppled out of the nest, it was a puff of feathers on the ground.

In her younger days, she'd have run to its rescue, climbed a tree to find its home, or scoured the house for a suitable box. Feed the thing until it could fly or it died. These days, she left the lost birds alone. Saving them was an exercise in futility. They either ended up back on the ground or would die on her watch no matter how hard she tried to keep them alive. Without parents and a proper home, they rarely survived.

Catherine studied the wide-eyed little robin, stock still in the grass. She laughed. It reminded her of one of her students—must've been twenty years ago—who arrived in her classroom like a frightened baby bird. Joan, with wispy blond hair that stood like static on the top of her head, started out shy and almost in shock in her classroom. Her skinny legs barely held her up. Catherine hadn't known what to make of her.

Leaning on her spade, Catherine pictured herself: Miss Hathaway in her fifth-grade classroom, guiding students year after year to discover their exciting world. With countless hours of preparation, she designed her classes for maximum impact in the minimum window of attention. Ten- and eleven-year-olds had a way of zoning out just after lunch or right before the buses began lining up outside the windows in late afternoon. That's when she leaned in, reading the signals of interest and disinterest on her students' faces and bodies. She made an art of keeping their attention.

Science was Miss Hathaway's end-of-the-day remedy. In the afternoons she would bring out the hands-on lessons, using common ingredients to uncommon effect. Like mixing vinegar and baking soda to blow up a balloon, or food coloring and celery to transform ordinary leaves. She showed the children how everyday interactions could make a miracle. Other days, she pulled out her bug specimens and colored pencils, urging the kids to bring detail alive on the page. In her classroom, the basic elements revealed the stuff of life.

But when Joan arrived, Catherine held back from her, sweeping the room with her gaze to call on the confident children. The child stirred a fear in her that took weeks to unravel. Whenever a classmate or teacher spoke to her, Joan's body froze like a wild rabbit. The flood of chatter and commands from kids and adults alike had a muting effect on her energy and her mouth. She placed her words carefully when giving an answer, like picking a path through a minefield.

Late in the fall, after prompting Joan to tell the class about the butterfly she held in a jar, Catherine recognized herself in the student.

As the child explained how a caterpillar transformed from chrysalis to butterfly, becoming the dusty-winged thing in her palms, the girl Catherine appeared in the classroom. She mimicked Joan's manner of speaking, slow and succinct to avoid mistakes. Watching Joan brought a choking lump to Catherine's throat, as if she was seeing a painful part of her life all over again. And she recognized Joan's suffering.

"Miss Hathaway, can I give you a hug?" the girl said after Catherine congratulated her on her butterfly report. This uncharacteristic boldness brought her across the classroom to embrace the waif. Joan held so tightly for so long, tears gathered at the back of Catherine's eyes. From then on, reading Joan's face each morning, Catherine responded accordingly. If the little girl seemed somewhat relaxed and happy, she knew she could coax some creativity and courage out of her.

"Who would like to hold the praying mantis? Joan?"

If there was a shadowy tightness on her face, Catherine made sure Joan was close while the other kids measured ingredients for the lesson that day. Joan found her freedom in getting lost in the wonder of what was happening. Catherine found joy in helping the girl come alive in her classroom. Both had blossomed a bit by the end of the school year when their time together ended.

"Miss Hathaway, I love you," she said on the last day of school.

She squeezed the girl's hands in hers. "Joan, I will never forget you."

For many years after, Catherine stayed in touch with Joan as she grew into a teenager with many friends and lots of ambition. In fact, the last time she'd heard from her, Joan was a grown woman studying for her master's degree in biology.

Catherine jabbed absentmindedly at the soil. She had nearly forgotten her impact as a teacher. She had forgotten Joan's impact on her. Breaking up a few clods of earth, her body warming with the work, she decided to keep digging for treasured memories like Joan when the loneliness and confusion of old age threatened to bury her.

The robins resumed their alarm, drawing Catherine back to the shocked young bird on the ground. Sighing, she thrust the spade deeper into the soil and stepped past it toward the pathetic little thing. She bent over it, and the young robin fluttered up and away to a low branch, a fresh chorus of voices cheering from high in the tree. No need for her rescue after all. It had only needed a reason to fly—and the mama bird was certainly close by.

25. Mad Patty

"Miss Hathaway, what do you think you're doing, bringing my kid into your house and feeding her stuff?" The voice hammered the back of Catherine's head.

Patty marched across the grass to Catherine, who stood with a hand in her mailbox, feet still in her slippers. The heat and humidity had hit hard this mid-morning, and the young woman's face was florid. A strand of pink-streaked hair waved like an ugly feather on her head.

"What? I—what?" Catherine's cheeks flamed so hot, they seemed to melt from her face. "Well, I just thought . . . You know, she was crying and seemed so sad and hungry and I had—"

"*Don't* take her inside again. Okay, Miss Hathaway? I can barely keep track of her as it is. I can't be worrying about her being in a stranger's house."

"Stranger? Well, I'm hardly going to . . ." She touched the top of the mailbox to hide her wobbling.

"Look, I'm sorry, but,"—Patty's voice had softened to a rubber mallet—"Tazzy just told me she was in your kitchen a few days ago and it freaked me out. We had a weird thing happen with a neighbor at our last rental, and I just get a little nervous. That's part of the reason we moved. I'm doing my best to stay afloat here, so please don't add to my stress."

Catherine smoothed the front of her house dress, ironing wrinkles in the thin cotton. "Well, talking about stress, your daughter does seem to be a little, shall we say, shabby? And she often looks and acts like she's starving."

Patty's eyes widened. Her mouth fell open.

"And your son seems to be laboring under a heavy burden of responsibility." Catherine felt herself on a roll, somewhat out of control and possibly headed for a cliff. "He told me you've left him in charge of running the household."

Patty held her hands to the side of her head, her face flushing. "What? What are you talking about? I have been working my butt off to take *care* of my kids—not *burden* or hurt them." She stopped to take a deep breath, wheezing a little as she dragged her palms down to either side of her jaw. Sweat gathered on her forehead.

"Look." Catherine pressed on. "I don't know if you're a drinker, a smoker, or what you do when you're gone all of the time but—"

Patty interrupted. "*That* is none of your business!" She was shouting again and crying a little too, her tears mixing with the sweat dripping from her temples. "You have no idea what's going on in my life."

Catherine took a step back and tucked her chin to rise to her full height. Finding her confidence, she said, "It just seems like the children are suffering some neglect. And anyway, Tazzy comes into my yard without asking permission."

"I will make certain that my daughter does not come anywhere near your precious yard." Patty was in Catherine's face now, her eyes slits, her finger jabbing. "And you make sure you do not bring Tazzy into your house again."

Catherine's eyebrows shot up. Her rib cage deflated. She answered through clenched teeth. "I understand. I do. I will not be inviting your daughter into my home *ever* again."

Patty stomped off. Catherine's stomach somersaulted. She examined the envelopes in her shaking hand, until a screech drew her eyes to the sky.

A hawk soared above Patty's house, harried by three crows. A mockingbird called from her own rooftop, rehearsing its repertoire of secondhand songs.

The mail sailed from her hands when she slammed the box shut. Stooping to the curb, Catherine watched the heavy-set young woman wiggle her way into her Chevy, then back out of her driveway and into the street. The car's tires were bald, and the woman hadn't buckled her seat belt. Patty peeled away.

Catherine clutched her mail and hurried up the walk and into the house, her heart pounding, her neck as rigid as a tree trunk.

Doing her best to stay afloat— baloney!

She probably doesn't even buckle up those kids when they're in the car.

Where's she going and who's taking care of the children? Hardly seems right that a ten-year-old should be in charge of a little girl.

26. Mirror, Mirror

Catherine was mad. Steaming mad. She slammed into her bathroom, grabbed a washcloth, and soaked it in cold water. Lifting it dripping to her cheeks, she stared at herself in the mirror. The flush of her complexion enhanced the wrinkled and sagging places. The three-sided square between her brows was more prominent now. Her mouth turned down like a Greek tragedy mask, her hollow eyes curtained in translucent crepe.

You sure handled that conversation well, Old woman.

Never mind, Miss Catherine. You don't have to think about it ever again.

Catherine draped the cloth on the faucet and peered into the mirror. She struggled to squeeze more focus from her faded irises. The face frowning back at her was just an old woman—looking and acting the part.

When young, Catherine's skin was taut and seamless on high ivory cheekbones. It offset her imperfect nose and chin. She was an imposing statue poised to render a noisy classroom mute. Neither smiling nor frowning, she kept a steady gaze on her charges bobbing in a sea of desks. Like gulls on waves, becalmed and awed, they waited for her instructions.

In later years, she leaned toward the children, leaving her natural, neutral position. Didn't she warm to their unique needs and personality quirks? Couldn't she read their body language and engage them on emotional levels? She became a favorite with the kids, beloved to some.

Once upon a time, the mirror described the light in her eyes and the lift of her smile as somewhat becoming. She could still see the girl she had been. But now, as the rose in her cheeks paled to antique-white, the mirror only said, *What a mess you are.*

Catherine's fingers plowed the surface of her scalp, trying to work through the tangles. Her head stayed disheveled these days, a squirrel's nest of disarray.

"Why bother? No one notices." Her voice echoed in the spotless room. Stepping backward, she examined her figure at full length. The same old drape of a dress hung above the same sad slippers.

You've lost your self-respect, Old Woman.

Where's your flexibility, your go-with-the-flow, Miss Catherine?

Gone. Like the girl.

You could lean in, bend a bit, shift the trajectory.

Or close the gate and secure the locks. Who needs the drama?

Catherine rested her shoulder against the wall, closing her eyes. That Patty woman said she was strange. Didn't trust her with her daughter. How had it come to this?

She tried to summon some of her life's wisdom, but couldn't conjure a single platitude. Too many memories had fled her head. She kept her photo albums to prove she had lived. But the pictures felt familiar only because she scanned them again and again. The memories themselves were like old Polaroids, discolored and murky behind yellowed plastic. The sum of her life had not measured up to its parts.

Where had the time gone? Twenty-two years of a sputtering start, forty more of dogged teaching, a few spare moments of declining retirement. What a seven-decade piece of work she was.

She used to believe this blank slate of a brain was an answer to her childish prayer: Dear God, please erase the painful tapes playing in my head. Had the Almighty given her a break? The waking anguish had dissipated.

However, the images haunting her dreams persisted: always a baby crying, a river rushing, and a child she couldn't find to save her life.

And lately, through Fate's sleight of hand or Divine appointment, some memories were returning full force in broad daylight.

Catherine swiped at a tear and faced her reflection once more. She propped her forehead on the glass. Its coolness couldn't calm. All she saw were distorted features. Her nose grown lumpier, her upper lip stitched with tiny vertical lines. Her worst qualities getting worse, eclipsing the scant beauty she'd had.

What would become of her if she couldn't keep a civil relationship with a struggling neighbor, let alone a lonely child? What had she already become if not the nosy old lady she appeared to be from a stranger's point of view? From her point of view.

No use trying to turn over new leaves now.

No need to lose more than you already have.

Catherine pushed off from the mirror and settled her hips against the countertop. Taking one more look, she declared, "I can change. I can do better—do what's right. Forget the bending over backwards and going with the flow—I will stand up and do what I must." She powdered her nose and chin, pinned her hair to the top of her head, and went to make that phone call.

27. Risk and Fingerprints

The garbage truck rumbled like a hungry beast in the distance. Catherine stood transfixed in her front room, the sunlight ricocheting off of her polished mahogany tables and the glossy hardwood floors. She lifted the phone from its cradle and held it like a baby in her arms. She'd lost her resolve in the short walk from the bathroom to the sitting room. Returning the phone to its base, she gave herself some time. Have a quick snack, get the trash can in, maybe water a few plants.

She straightened a crooked print on the wall on her way to the kitchen. Having scooped a spoonful of yogurt into her favorite flowered bowl, she returned to the front room to eat and watch the mechanical monster devour her neighbors' trash.

A picture of Patty crossed her mind, the way she always saw her—a quick slam out the door, a hurried slide into the car, a careless backing out of the driveway. Catherine's heart pounded all over again. The kids were never with her. She came in late and left at odd hours. Probably went to a bar. An irresponsible mother who hung out with derelicts and ramshackle men.

Did Patty really care about her daughter that morning she went missing? She did threaten to hit her, Miss Catherine.

Go ahead and jump to conclusions, Old Woman. Don't hold any of your horses.

Tazzy's arm was throbbing red, like she was grabbed too hard.

Hard to tell what's too hard and what's just how hard it is.

A bottle escaped Patty's garbage can. It fell as the truck was gobbling it up. The clear glass container made its getaway down the sloping road toward Catherine's driveway. After the dinosaur rumbled off, she put her bowl in the sink and went to collect her empty can. Letting the door slam behind her, she strode first to the curb where the thing had landed.

An empty whiskey bottle. She could've guessed it.

She pinched its neck and lifted it like a snake caught hiding in a woodpile. Holding it out for inspection, Catherine let the ladies find her resolve.

An obvious remnant of trouble and abuse. Mother had done her worst when the bottle was empty.

Time to make that call. Before the children get hurt—or worse.

A mixture of diesel fumes and rotted food invaded Catherine's nose. Her stomach flip-flopped all the way up the front walk. Her reflection in the window glass barely registered, though her hair had come loose from its clip and become a matted mess. Sweat streamed down the sides of her face and off the tip of her nose. But she had other things on her mind.

Back in the kitchen, she deposited the whiskey bottle into the recycling bin. With shaking hands, she picked up the phone. She knew who to call. She had the number ready. Her training as a teacher told her this was her duty, her job. She'd never done it. Never risked making the mistake of being mistaken.

Catherine punched in the numbers with one steady finger. Just an anonymous call from a neighbor who cared, a neighbor who had her suspicions. She wasn't exactly making an accusation, just requesting an investigation. Determine if the family needed help.

She guessed that the Child Protective Services people would knock on Patty's door and look for signs of abuse. They will probably say, *You know, there are many resources for moms—people—in need of help from time to time. Food vouchers and classes for parenting and . . .* Why wouldn't Patty want someone to help? Maybe she just needed a shove in the right direction.

Catherine would never forgive herself if something bad happened to this child. The kid had left fingerprints all over her heart.

Summer

I know the bottom, she says.
I know it with my great tap root:
It is what you fear.
I do not fear it: I have been there.

—Sylvia Plath, *Elm*

28. A Day to Forget

Weeks ago, when the CPS people pulled up, Catherine was perched on her front porch with Percy at her feet. He sensed they were outsiders the second they left their car. Brisk steps, then crisp knocks on Patty's door elicited low growls from his throat.

Catherine nabbed him and slipped inside. But she had not been quick enough. Patty locked eyes with her over the shoulders of the two strangers standing there.

From behind a curtain, Catherine watched the three of them in the doorway. Patty clasping her hands to her chest as she listened wide-eyed to what the women were saying. Patty shaking her head, stricken as she stepped back to allow them in. They didn't stay long, though the door had closed.

Catherine hovered at the window. She wondered if the social workers saw or even spoke to the children. She was certain that her neighbor had seen and read through her like a book when their eyes met in that split second. Patty knew who had done the deed.

Better get moving, Old Woman. Stewing doesn't do any good.

Don't give it another thought, Miss Catherine.

As she hoed between the rows of okra in her garden, Catherine's mind rolled over and over in an agitated stream. The little girl, Tazzy, had been invisible these past weeks since Patty had told her to stay away.

Was it a mistake, making that call? Would Catherine ever discover if her suspicions were justified, if she had helped in some way, now that the lines of communication were severed? She wished she could reverse the clock and rework some avenues of her life. She wondered what the mother told her daughter.

Her brow furrowed, she stopped to examine her crop. The okra was dying, and she didn't know why. Not enough water or too much heat? She chopped the weeds hiding beneath the mulch. Suddenly, her arms and legs became rubber. Her vision blurred as if something strange were happening to her.

Untethered was the word that flickered in her head like an old fluorescent bulb. Leaning on the hoe, she wiped her forehead with her bandana.

Not much of a birthday you're having today, Miss Catherine.

One day's the same as any other day, Old Woman.

Too bad you never forget this one day.

Yeah, because birthdays are for babies.

Her stomach dropped, urging her legs to move. Catherine settled heavily on her bench in the shade. Sixty-one years ago, Mother had forgotten her birthday.

That scorching summer day was hotter than any she could remember.

She was up early, unable to sleep and already sweating. The bedroom had a tiny window that always yawned open, held aloft with a stray piece of molding. But the room stayed stuffy at night, especially since the fan on the floor had stopped working. Mother said to get over it and sleep on top of the sheets.

The girl Catherine was turning ten and trying to feel her double digits. Closing her eyes, all she felt was sticky and hungry. Saturday morning and Mother wasn't home yet. She probably stayed out with some guy for her Friday night fun after work.

Mother had been steady at her job lately and had gotten a handle on her drinking ever since the government people had visited. She and Catherine had found a settled rhythm for running the household this summer: Mother worked and partied while Catherine cared for their sweet Baby June.

But on her birthdays, Mother always gave her a card with some cash or left a note somewhere saying, "Happy Birthday, Catherine."

Not this time.

The air conditioner squatted in the kitchen window, unplugged and unused as usual. Catherine's feet felt glued to the floor. Should she wake her little sister to help celebrate her day? Turning ten was a big deal to her and to the kids at school who invited her to their parties throughout the year. Baby June would catch her excitement, especially if her fever had subsided in the night.

She'd been born early and underweight. The poor infant was sick a lot. Catherine cared for her through many stuffed-up-nose nights and upset-tummy days.

"Take good care of your kid sister, Catherine Hathaway. We don't want the government to take her away from us, do we?"

Mother's question punctuated every decision the girl made: Ask to sleep at a friend's or stay home with Baby June? Grab an hour for reading or read to Baby June? Love and guilt fused in her bones like conjoined twins. She couldn't fathom their separation.

Mother was happy yesterday afternoon, putting on makeup and fixing her hair for work. "I gotta get to the restaurant and keep the rent money coming. You and Baby June can eat those frozen chicken nuggets for supper tonight, Catherine. Just heat them in the oven. There's a jar of peas in the fridge, too."

The girl Catherine liked standing in the leftover steam from the shower, breathing in the mixture of hot-curling-iron-and-hairspray smells making the bathroom thick and sticky. Mother clicked her compact shut and pressed past her in the doorway. Hurrying through the hall, she called over her shoulder. "If her cold gets worse, get her to blow her nose before bed. And keep the covers off her. I think she's got a little fever."

Catherine had fed Baby June and put her to bed early that evening. She wasn't really a baby anymore. Her kid sister was thirteen months old by then and getting harder to handle. She was all over the place, pulling up and mostly walking. Catherine was in charge because school was out, and the lady who did daycare in her apartment downstairs wanted too much money.

Just before the front door slammed, Catherine heard, "There's some donuts in the freezer for your breakfast and some cereal in the cabinet, too. Don't eat it all. And don't wait up for me tonight."

As the morning sun drilled in through the kitchen window, the girl Catherine closed her eyes for a second, pretending cold air from the vents was lifting the hair off her neck. She rummaged for the used birthday candles in the junk drawer while she waited for the frozen donuts to thaw and for Baby June to wake up. When she'd checked her earlier, she was sound asleep under her covers. The little girl rarely slept this long, but the head cold and slight fever must have made her tired.

"Probably just sleeping it off," she said out loud to move the stifling air.

That's something Mother would say. Catherine smirked, twisting the waxy pink candle with the blackened wick between her fingers.

Just sleeping it off. How many times had Mother mumbled it when Catherine needed her to get up?

Her voice was loud that morning: "I will not be like my mother." It was her solemn oath, the empty kitchen her witness.

Double-digit Catherine felt suddenly old, the apartment's atmosphere dense and leaden. A wave of panic rose, then collapsed in her chest. Her stomach lurched at the smell of sticky donuts and waxy plastic. The apartment was too still, too quiet.

Like a wet load of laundry after a broken spin cycle, her body refused to be moved. She lifted her legs one at a time and stumbled down the hall. The bedroom's dismal beige walls glowed with unusual yellow-gold. She gently shook Baby June in her crib. No movement. The blanket and sheets wrapped themselves around her neck and face. Heavy and choking. Baby June's body was cool, moist flesh in the heat. No breath on her lips. The girl Catherine clawed the layers away. June's eyes were closed, her face peaceful.

Catherine remembered screaming, shaking her sister, then lifting her from the tangle of sweaty blankets. A dead baby's body, heavy forever on her big sister's chest.

29. Moving On

The July rain arrived without warning. Large, plopping drops peppered Catherine, pasting her clothes to her skin. She kept at it with the hoe, chopping the sticky clay soil, killing weeds. Some of the okra fell with them.

The skies were a steady shower now, pelting the trees and battering the earth into puddles. What a birthday. She thought she had put that terrible day out of her mind. Hadn't dug up her history in years. June had just come and gone. Or so she had believed.

Why didn't you use the air conditioner when Mother wasn't home?

Where were the neighbors? They must've known you were always alone.

Why didn't you tell the social workers that you needed help?

How did you miss how sick your poor sister was?

"When the temperature's always running high, how does a girl know what's normal and what's boiling over?" Catherine's voice boomed from her chest, but the soggy air muted it, refused to carry it. Using both hands, she raised the hoe above her head and flung it with all of her strength.

Could she have saved Baby June? If she'd checked her in the middle of the night when she kicked off her own blankets, could she have eased her burning fever and suffocating cold? Or was her body just too weak to handle any more suffering?

Catherine could never answer her own questions.

After Baby June was gone, she lived with strangers. The government lady, Miss Baker, who gave her the card with the number to call, was kind. She answered all her questions about the foster family.

"They have six kids: two biological, two adopted, and two fosters like you. You'll be the oldest and they are so excited to meet you. Any other questions?"

"When will I get to go back home with Mother?"

"As soon as your mother gets herself in good shape again, Catherine."

But instead of getting in shape, her mother went downhill fast, like a stick shift in neutral with no brakes. She lost her job, lost the apartment, ended up in a shelter, disappeared into herself, and never came looking for her barely breathing, barely living daughter, Catherine. Eventually, she vanished altogether. Miss Baker said Mother was probably living on the street somewhere.

For her part, young Catherine disrupted out of home after home, family after family. Her body numb, her mind detached, she did not know how disruptive her wildness was at the time. Some of the families were good people trying to make a safe haven for a lost little girl. Others were just filling their rooms for the monthly extras. And then all of the foster families in between.

But she was only conscious of the walls closing in with living, breathing little kids wherever she lived. And strange adults with confusing new rules. Other people's "normal" surrounding her stunned senses, her shattered core. The woods and bushes and streams constantly called her away, and she followed. The angry or frightened parents said it wasn't safe.

"You've got to stay inside where we can take care of you. You can't keep running away."

But she did. Much later, when filling out forms for college, Catherine learned to say she'd become a social orphan in her teens. Because her living parent had given up on life and the foster care system was unable to contain her, Catherine had landed at a residential center.

When she arrived at the Plover Home Cottages, the loss of her family had already dissolved something in her essence. Her tears had dried and transformed her heart of flesh to rock salt, leaving behind a heavy residue of something rigid and crystallized.

However, after a few years, young Catherine came alive to more than mere survival. As if waking from a nightmare in a slow-motion crawl, she began to accept from the house parents and the Plover Home's programs much of what they wanted to bestow. With other un-adopted, disruptive teenagers, she learned to tend a vegetable garden, mend fences and furnaces, and get help from outside sources. Her years in the Plover Home cottages filled the gaps and stretched the length of time needed for maneuvering through adolescence into young womanhood.

Catherine was seventeen and beginning to recognize her own skin, to feel herself filling in the shell of her extra-tall frame like a hot-air balloon suffusing with heat.

"So, you think you'd be a good teacher?" The woman was gentle and kept her eyes locked on Catherine's, her manicured hands resting on the desk.

Catherine held her gaze. "I don't know but I want to try. I like learning and I think I'd enjoy helping little kids." She brushed a hand across her own perfectly polished fingernails.

"All right, Catherine, good. There are programs to help young people like you get into college, find financial aid, move on to a productive life."

She had taken to college like any normal eighteen-year-old: struggling with her independence and with making friendly connections over the course of four years. After graduating with honors, she became Miss Hathaway, teaching kindergarten the following autumn. Leaving the girl Catherine behind, she moved on to becoming the woman she wanted to be.

But today, as Catherine worked in the pounding rain, she sensed a loosening of deeply compacted dirt, the stirring up of settled silt, a shift in the resistance at her core. This unmooring, a relentless tug that threatened to uproot her, she could neither name nor ignore.

Moving on from here, it was hers to decide if the flood would swallow and sweep her away. Or if it would force her to dig in deeper, stretch higher, and bend more than ever. Could she learn to go with the flow and embrace whatever the weather brought her way?

30. Chance and Circumstance

The afternoon sun hammered the asphalt, boiling the morning's rain away. A low layer of steam hovered above the road. Catherine drove the speed limit, paying careful attention to both sides of the scenic highway. The mown grass along the edges was sending up fresh shoots and enticing deer to nibble. The beautiful creatures had no sense when it came to cars. She saw a dead doe on her way to the eye doctor and didn't want to add to the carnage now on the drive home.

Dr. Morton had run her through the tests. He declared she was lucky she had needed no more than reading glasses up this point. But her luck had run out.

"Yes, Miss Hathaway, you are experiencing some age-related vision changes. Your eyes have been compensating well until now. I think we could attribute your dizziness and tripping to depth perception issues."

Catherine snickered at his words. "More like death perception. The older I get, the more I can see my impending death."

Dr. Morton chuckled, slid his chair back, and reached to flick on the overhead lights. "Yes, but at least the end will be in sight." Catherine rolled her eyes and smiled, glad he'd matched her clumsy joke.

He tilted his head sideways, kindness in his smile. "You know, Miss Hathaway, the lenses in our eyeballs become rigid as we age. This prescription could make a world of difference for you; you'll see better than you have in years. Maybe even find your balance again."

He had also taken photos of the backs of both eyes and assured her he would call if he saw any problems with her retinas.

"I saved a man from brain cancer last summer, my dear. If he had skipped his yearly exam, I would not have found that malignant tumor near his eye."

Catherine promised to make regular visits. Although she bristled at his indiscreet suggestions of catastrophe. He had continued his speech. "You can replace a kidney and even receive a new heart. But if you lose your vision—well, you can't fix blindness, can you? Take care."

He handed her a small piece of paper scrawled with mysterious symbols and chicken scratch. She delivered the cryptic instructions to his assistant after choosing the least-obtrusive frames. The helpful young lady offered to mail them, save Catherine the return trip. She claimed they'd arrive in just over a week.

"When you get the glasses, try them out for a few days. They may disorient you at first, but before you know it, you'll feel like a brand-new woman. And if they need adjusting, just come back to see us." Catherine nodded, though she was certain she'd be looking and feeling older than ever.

Driving home in the afternoon heat, she blinked at the blacktop. It radiated in waves that distorted the road. She slowed and glanced at the dead doe she'd passed earlier. It was covered with unabashed vultures. Up ahead on the right, a cluster of deer grazed along the highway's berm. She touched the brake, keeping them in her sights.

A movement to the left drew her attention. Before she could think, a young doe bounded in front of her car. Catherine slammed her foot to the floor, engaging the antilock brakes and clipping the confused animal on its right hind flank. The far edge of her bumper spun the small doe in a complete circle, rear legs splaying and sliding, then finding traction after skittering ten feet from the car.

Catherine pulled over to the shoulder, her hands shaking, her heart pounding. The frightened animal ran full speed in the direction of the trees and disappeared into the woods.

She inhaled sharply then exhaled sobbing. Deluged with a jumbled mixture of relief and grief, she pressed her face against her knuckles on the steering wheel.

"I tried to be careful. I did everything I could. I don't know what else I could have done." She sat in her car on the side of the road for an eternity, waiting for the fist in her chest to release. She said in a whisper, "I did my best. What else I could have done? I did my best. What else I could have done?"

Finally, she raised her head and scanned the tree line. No sign of the doe. The other animals were gone, too.

Clinging to the wheel, she looked at the sky and thanked heaven she hadn't done more damage. The doe would most likely be fine.

31. Ageless

Catherine's eyes popped open. A coyote howl. Her dream had absorbed the first yipping barks. But the throaty yowls coming from the open bedroom window had cut through her sleep. Her cheek rested against the pillow. The clock threw a glowing green five across the room. She'd had that dream again.

Blackest night. She stands at the threshold of the back door. First, the snakes rippling through the yard. Orange-diamonded ribbons muscling toward the creek. Then the alligators. Crashing beasts in the brush on the far bank. Wolves and foxes follow the path, chasing each other or passing along the track. The creek below teems with shark-sized carp. Whales and rays lumber through, shiny gray-black bodies half-exposed in the rushing waterway.

Catherine is afraid. Always afraid in this dream. She is safe from the creatures, but a cry rises from the creek. A child. Catherine cannot move. Always only watching wordless and frozen while the river surges.

Five a.m. and Catherine was wide awake, trembling in sweat. Throwing off the heavy comforter that never left her bed, she lay in the half light. Remembering.

Tonight's version of her recurring dream had an added element. She had moved from her doorway.

Lying in the dark, Catherine willed the images to replay in her brain.

Following the animal parade, Catherine stumbles outside. The night blinds her. She sidesteps an enormous snake. Follows it down, down the slope. She searches for something, someone. Sobs wrack her body. Disconnected from thoughts, she tastes the grief. Rushing water, wind from its wake. Lost, lost, the water hisses, wet breath on her face.

She reaches the willow. Throws her arms about her great waist.

The animals recede. Catherine knows only the tree. And her roots exposed at her feet. And the branches umbrella-ing. Catherine spins. A pale blue glow lights this lovely willow chamber. Slender branches circle and kiss the damp earth. Her feet sink in the spongey moss. She bends to caress its emerald textures. Her hands are young.

Fear snatches at her throat. She swallows a cry. She stands, trips backward outside the drape of cascading leaves. In her retreat, they scrape her cheeks, a shoal of silver-green minnows. She is dizzy, disoriented. Frozen in shadowy darkness once more. An outsider, interloper. Afraid to stay, afraid to go.

Come.

She parts the willow branches again. Into the sanctuary. The light casts shadows. Steps etch the tree trunk. Catherine must climb.

Up, up, up. She senses her strength. Higher, higher, she's close to the top.

A leafy veil; Catherine sweeps the screen aside. A face lined and rustic, a web of surface cracks. Catherine touches weathered skin, a crepe-paper face. Eyes hollow yet piercing, wrinkled deltas on either side joining seas of silver-gray, waving about deep carved temples and pounding with the night wind. Hiding and highlighting what was and is and will be.

Catherine leans back. A statue alive. Her fingers claw and cling to this armor of bark. Her arms link with branches on either side. Her feet rest on calloused shoulders, her spine settles on a vertical limb, solid yet supple for bending in the wind. It speaks, the face faded in textures of time. Ageless and patient.

"Follow the cry," it whispers like wind.

"I'm afraid," says the woman within the willow.

"You have everything you need," hums from her trunk.

"No, something is missing!" she wants to shriek.

"You know everything you need," rumbles from her core.

"But I don't know how to live. What do I need?"

"You will know when you know it. It has always been with you."

The dawn glowed behind the bedroom blinds, outlining the edges then spreading to include the walls and ceiling. As daylight added definition to the room, Catherine lost most of the dream's details. The edge of the bed held her, suspended, toes grazing the floor. The ageless face scrambled away from her clutching memory. Willow branches and snakes writhed in her periphery. Heaviness clung to her gut. Long after the dream vanished, her throat throbbed with grief and hope.

32. Flood

Catherine's gardening overalls gathered cobwebs as she plowed through the piles of boxes and assorted artifacts clogging her garage. The stench of mildew was driving her crazy and she had to find its source.

She pushed aside a stack of plastic bins filled with old clothing she'd never wear again. She shoved the greasy lawnmower waiting patiently for its repair. She slid a metal shelf sideways, her years of accumulated teaching tools tottering before settling. The path clear, she shuffled toward the far wall, where a small window allowed enough daylight to expose the dust floating everywhere.

Looming up through the haze was the culprit: a cardboard box slumped against the cinder block. A damp circle on the concrete floor surrounded the box. A moist crack in the outer wall behind it meant a slow leak had rotted the thing. Mother's old clothing showed through a ruptured corner at the bottom. Splotches of black-green fungus covered part of the wall and most of the cardboard.

Catherine sneezed. She'd have to clear out those old things, spray some bleach, and get someone out here to fix the cracked concrete. Hands on her hips, she willed the muscles in her shoulders to stop contracting. She lowered her chin to her chest to stretch the back of her neck. A shiny object in the dusty sunlight caught her eye.

A key. She bent to retrieve the little thing flattening itself against the floor, camouflaged in matching gray. No wonder she'd missed it before. She slid a fingernail under its thin body and pinched it between her thumb and forefinger. Not much to it, just a cheap piece of metal, but it would probably do the trick.

The lock still hung on the gate, looped to the latch, waiting to fulfill its duty should the key ever materialize. Seems it had.

Catherine sneezed again, wiped her nose on her sleeve, and slipped the key into her front bib pocket. She approached the decaying box and poked the rotted corner with her toe. It collapsed open, leaving a pile of moldy clothes at her feet and a cloud of mildew in her nostrils.

Here's your real problem, Old Woman. Mother's leavings are coming back to haunt you.

Haven't looked in this box of hers in eons. Wonder what's in here.

Same stuff as the last time you looked, nearly forty years ago. Just throw it all away.

Sometimes you don't know what you have until you need it.

Catherine laughed at the puzzling déjà vu and added, "Sometimes you know what you need when you find it."

She sifted through the pile of Mother's musty old blouses and slacks. A familiar-looking hardback book surfaced beneath the clothing stack. Catherine lifted it and brushed a hand across the cover.

The Girl at the Gate. She touched the pencil-and-watercolor drawing of a child beside a broad ivy-laced gate. A white pinafore and pink bow framed her grin. Her hand was on the latch.

Catherine remembered this book. She'd devoured the stories as a kid, pleading with Mother to read it to her until she could read it over and over herself. The adventures of a young girl who began each chapter with her hand on the latch. Paused in the gateway, the girl encountered the question of staying in or going out. Not a coming-of-age narrative but rather a returning to the wisdom of innocence, the vignettes chronicled the girl's game of striking a balance between choosing the places of comfort at home and chancing the unknown places she could go.

The Girl at the Gate brought life to the girl Catherine.

Hugging the book, she scooted from the garage to the kitchen. She filled her tea kettle at the sink then plunked down at the table to wait for the water to boil. She flipped through the familiar pages, recalling how she'd followed that girl, answered the call to adventure with her, risking missteps, facing dangers. And escaping Mother's anger and neglect.

The tumult of years, however, had swept the book from her. The fiction faded and reality left her in the dust. She was surprised her mother had managed to hold onto this treasure despite her own setbacks and upheavals.

Children's voices floated into the kitchen through the open window. Must be the neighbor kids. Catherine imagined herself reading the stories to that Tazzy girl. "Nope," she said. "Not gonna happen."

Percy's ears perked and his eyes met hers.

"Just talking to myself again, sweet Pup." She smiled and leaned to pet his butterscotch head. The book slid from her lap, landed on its spine, and loosened from the binding where the glue had crumbled. Its pages splayed where it lay. Percy came sniffing to see what had fallen.

A small pink notecard had skittered across the floor. She bent to retrieve it, suddenly disjointed. Her mother's handwriting scrawled inside the card:

Dear Catherine,

I hope you find this note inside your book when you come to get my things.

They tell me I am very sick and may not live long.

I want to say I'm sorry.

I am sorry for not being a good mother. I hope you can forgive me.

There were circumstances, which I could never explain, that made me the way I am, made your childhood the way it was. My own growing up was confusing at best and quite terrifying at worst. But that's not yours to know about or to hold. And it's no excuse.

I could have done better.

Just know, I always loved you and your sister, although it may not have seemed so. I was trying to take care of you two and have some life for myself. But I didn't know how to live at all after Baby June died.

Seems I could never find the happiness and peace I was looking for. I hope you have found yours.

Sincerely,
Mother

A rush of heat raised the hair on Catherine's head. The kettle began to sing its low but rising siren. She straightened and steadied her shoulders against the back of the chair. How had she missed this message for all of these years? How had a letter so precious been hidden for so long? What did it mean that she had found it now?

She drifted in slow motion from the chair to the stove, twisting off the burner as Percy fled the screaming kettle. It exhaled with a slow whimper. Catherine crumpled to the floor, her back against the oven door, the cool hardwood a welcome support.

Tears gathered in the creases of her eyes, rolled down the sides of her cheeks and along the ridges of her chin, then dripped to her chest. Her body heaved as she sobbed and sobbed and sobbed.

What had begun as a trickle widened to a stream. Expelled by underground pressure, egged on by gravity, the flow rushed to become a waterfall that grew into a river moving through all her hidden and hollow places, washing across wide valleys of sorrow and chasms of loss.

The dam had burst. Long-slumbering energies rumbled to the surface for a well-deserved surge. The gates were open. It had begun. A purging, dissolving, unstoppable flood.

33. Overflow

Catherine's toes squished with every step of her inspection of the roses. The blooms sagged beneath the weight of the heavy rainfall. She had never seen the yard get this flooded. But storms had been moving through for several days, turning the lawn to a swamp. Assessing the dark skies to the west, she guessed more was on the way. She slogged through the soggy grass to examine the succulents in the hanging basket fastened to her gate. A bit drowned but nothing she could do about them now.

A shout lured Catherine to the hole in her fence.

"Don't go anywhere near that creek today, Tazzy. It's running high and probably stronger than it looks." Patty was on her porch, yelling into the house through the open door. "Patrick, keep an eye on your sister." She let the door slam and huffed down the steps to her car.

Catherine swung her eyes to the dark brown line at the far edge of her yard. The creek tumbled over rocks and roots it rarely touched. Its roar prickled her skin. She had to see what the fuss was all about.

"C'mon, Percy, let's find out what the rain did to our little creek."

She retrieved her heavy-duty rubber boots from the closet. The little dog spun in circles by the door. She slid into the boots and grabbed her walking stick. Plodding along through the muddy yard, they made their way to the swollen stream.

At the water's edge beneath the willow, Catherine's jaw dropped. It was as if a giant aquarium had collapsed upstream, its insides spilling out and racing to freedom regardless of objects in its path. The rough plank on the low bank where she sometimes sat had washed away. The stepping-stones where she and Percy often crossed were six inches below the surface, except the tallest one, which still held its flat head an inch above the flow. Long white fangs fanned out over rocks where small ripples of water had cautiously circled before. Some of the weeping willow's gnarled toes had disappeared beneath the surface. The tree was trailing multiple fingers in the muddy stream, her limbs excited in the tugging energy.

Percy sniffed along the bank, eyeing the spot where he liked to wade into the water.

"No, Percy, come!" Her sharp tone pricked his ears. He looked at her face, considering his options, then dashed toward her, sensing her fear. "You haven't had any practice swimming in water like this," she explained, scratching his back.

Her eyes fled downstream. She gasped as a large log tumbled like a twig under the water's force. Was it her cedar-log bridge that had just taken the plunge? She craned her neck upstream.

No, there it lay across the creek. Normally a foot above the surface, her makeshift bridge had become one with the water. A thin waterfall fanned out in silver-white bangs from the top of the log where it bumped up against the stream.

"We won't be crossing that bridge today, Percy." Catherine patted the side of her thigh, and he followed her back up to the house.

Later that afternoon as the mailman sped from her curb and splashed up the road, Catherine clomped down the driveway to her mailbox, still wearing her sturdy boots. When she reached to retrieve the usual envelopes and advertisements, her knuckles bumped the small package shoved to the back. She smiled at the box—her new glasses! She had expected them to take months to arrive, but sure enough, here they were in just over a week.

Back in the house, she examined herself in the front room mirror. Behind the brown-green tortoise shell frames snug against her temples, her face didn't look so bad. Some aspects were a bit too conspicuous, like the tiny wrinkles on the bottom rim of her eyes. But others were somewhat reassuring, like the softness in those familiar blue irises and the strands of pure silver framing her face. She toured the room, pleased that the textures and patterns of her curtains and pillows were crisp with definition. Even her framed lilac print revealed details she had never noticed. She clutched the back of a chair. She'd have to wait and see if the balance improved and the dizziness disappeared.

Someone banged on her front door. Percy started barking. Catherine followed him to see who it was now mashing the bell.

Glasses perched high on her nose, she opened the door a crack. The boy Patrick stared back at her while the dog barked crazily.

"Stop, Percy, stop! Patrick, what's wrong?" His face was paler than she'd ever seen.

"Tazzy's gone—I can't find her," he squeezed out between breaths. "Mom just got home and is looking for her on the other side of the neighborhood. She told me to come get you."

Catherine slammed out the door with Percy at her side. They followed the boy toward his backyard.

"When did you notice she was missing? Where have you looked?" Her mind was flying to the creek as her legs kept stride beside the boy.

"She was with me all day but went out to play after lunch. I was watching her through the window while I played my video game. But then I got caught up in it . . ." Catherine glanced at him as they walked. Patrick's face sagged, his mouth tugging down and his eyes filling with tears. "When Mom got home, I realized she was gone."

They reached the back patio where he said Tazzy had been playing princess with her dolls. Both of them scanned the far yards and looked to the woods beyond the roiling, muddy creek. Nothing. No one.

Catherine swayed in agitation. "Let me think. Did you see if she went toward the creek or the road?"

"No, I didn't see her leave the patio at all." He tucked his chin, blond bangs shadowing his face.

A tiny flapping of pink fabric caught Catherine's eyes. It fluttered far, far down the yard, across the creek. Percy saw it too and froze, his tongue hanging out and his tail wagging with uncertainty. There, where Catherine's rain-darkened fence met the water-logged bridge, was the little girl, preparing to come across from the other side.

"Tazzy, stop—Tazzy!" Catherine shouted, glued to the earth. The girl wasn't looking at her. Cupping her mouth, Catherine willed her voice to travel. "I'll come get you." It wouldn't carry that far. Too much distance between them.

Patrick saw his sister, too. One foot on the log, the other on the bank, her arms swam in the air, her body swinging like a pendulum.

"No, Tazzy, no!" Patrick ran toward the girl, and Percy took off with him, racing ahead. Catherine slid her new glasses back up the slope of her nose. She could see how this was going to go.

The bank was crumbling. Catherine's stomach dropped. The girl's foot sank slow-motion into the creek, her other foot slipping from the log. Tazzy twisted, her hands clawing the rough roots on the shore, both feet consumed by the thirsty water.

Catherine was a statue facing the forces of nature, paralyzed by the expanse between her and the girl and powerless to move a muscle.

The torrent tugged at the child's waist and dragged her hands from solid ground. All at once she was covered up to her chin and drifting toward the middle of the swollen creek. Percy and Patrick had reached the edge, both motionless as Tazzy traveled.

Catherine registered a seismic shift. It moved the solid ground beneath her and rolled up her spine, forcing a groan from her gut. She took two steps toward the girl, miles away from her now it seemed. She stopped as the water swept the child against the log bridge. Caught her breath as the girl caught it in a one-armed hug, her pale face hovering above the dark wood. Catherine ran in the opposite direction even as Percy darted out onto the unstable log.

She ran as fast as she could. Back through the side yards. Down the short path and through her gate. She grabbed her stick on the way, using it to pick up the pace. Over her wide lawn. Along the sloping hill. Down, down she struggled in the long journey to the low spot below the willow. Before it was too late.

Poised at the water's edge where she'd warned Percy off this morning, Catherine spied her dog on the log, fifty yards upstream. The girl's arm circled it still, her forehead a patch of white above panicked eyes. Catherine, thankful for the clear vision her glasses provided, stepped into the flow, gripping her walking stick. Her boots found the submerged stones, familiar in their feel though shrouded by the volume and force of the water.

The log bridge wobbled with the weight of Tazzy and Percy, its resting places giving way in tiny mudslides.

The bridge was becoming a boat.

In seconds the girl and the dog would be taking a slow, violent ride with or without the nebulous help of the dead cedar now releasing its hold on the earth.

Patrick's eyes were wild. He squinted at Catherine planted in the middle of the water far downstream. He stepped closer to the teetering log to which his sister clung. Catherine waved him back with wide sweeps of her free arm. "No," she said softly inside the roar. "Don't try it, Patrick. I'll catch her."

As if he heard, he backed up a foot. The log shifted another inch from the bank. Tazzy lifted her chin to discern where she and Percy were headed. She spotted Catherine.

"Willow, Willow, help. Help!" Her tiny cry hovered like a hummingbird between them.

The log broke free. Buoyant, it rolled, shaking Tazzy and the dog loose, ricocheting its way toward Catherine. The child was not far behind, her bottom end skipping and skimming over rough rocks while her head, hands, and feet took turns staying above water.

Catherine plunged her stick deeper into the creek, the stones under her threatening to let go of her rubber soles. She squared off with the river, her legs wide, knees slightly bent, and readied herself for however the child would arrive.

"Tazzy, it's okay! I'll catch you!" But the log reached her first. It lumbered into her knees and swept the hickory stick from her grip, carrying it away downstream. Thrown off balance, Catherine clawed the air for stability, shoulders and hips negotiating with gravity. Her back arched and chin thrust upward.

The willow's fingers dangled just above her head.

As if in a dream, Catherine reached toward the thin, bunched branches. Silver-green leaves dropped down to brush her palm, rope-like branches entwined her fingers. She squeezed the papery leaves and branches as they wrapped her wrist, suspending her above the tugging water. Her hold on the tree became the tree's hold on her.

The world is silent. Time slows. The woman Catherine finds the girl's face bobbing toward her in terror. Water pounds without sound. She tilts to where the girl will arrive at her knees, stretches out her free hand. Her heart sinks: her knees won't fold, she cannot reach the child. She leans in again, heavy with grief, willing her weight to bend the high branch.

Trembling above her, the branch allows her to crouch just as the child tumbles into her, choking and flailing, young eyes possessed with fear. Their flesh connects, wrist on wrist, fingernails into forearms. The woman Catherine hauls the girl up and out and to her side, one arm still rooted in the tree above. She drags them both along the underwater path to the bank. Catherine's boots connect with the solid earth, and the willow lets go. Two souls collapse onto the marshy sod.

Time passes then turns back to meet the soaked and shivering bodies of Catherine and Tazzy, clinging to each other on the ground.

Tazzy is crying, wrapped around Catherine. Catherine weeps with her, tears pouring with each wracking sob. The girl is all right. The girl is alive.

34. Adjustments

Patrick sprinted down the slope, his expression a mix of relief and shame.

Catherine waved him closer, reassuring him that Tazzy was safe. He fell to his knees, crying and hugging his sad little sister. The three of them held each other until time passed by again and led them to stand and wipe their eyes.

The hair stood up on Catherine's head. Where was Percy? Leaving a hand on Tazzy, she scanned in all directions. He could swim but that current was too much for him. How could she have forgotten about her precious dog? Her heart pounded like a drum inside her head.

"Percy, Percy." Catherine stared downstream and choked back tears.

"Mom, Mom." Tazzy stepped from the drape of her brother's arm and ran toward the house.

Patrick watched his sister race up the slope, and Catherine followed his gaze.

Patty hovered in the open gate with Percy in her arms. Discovering them all, the young woman gasped and ran down the hill. The dog wriggled free, passed Tazzy, and bolted for Catherine.

Patty arrived seconds behind him carrying her daughter. "My God, oh my God, Tazzy, where were you?" Tears streamed down the mother's face as she embraced the soaked child. All five creatures were shaking now.

The girl burst out, "Mom, I'm sorry, I went to see a lost baby deer in the woods across the creek, and when I came back, the bridge was slipping and I fell in . . ." She was crying again.

The boy stood with hands in his pockets. "Mom, I'm sorry. I should have been watching her. She could've drowned, but Miss Hathaway saved her." He pointed to the water beneath the willow.

Catherine had pulled back from their small huddle. She stood behind them, enveloping Percy's soaked and shaking body. "I'm so glad you're all right, you little drowned rat." She buried her face in his neck, loving him more than ever.

Patty turned to Catherine, still clutching her daughter and breathing hard. "Oh my God, Catherine, thank you. I don't know what would have happened if you hadn't been here." She settled Tazzy back on the ground, hugging her again.

"We don't have to think about what *didn't* happen." Catherine smiled, squeezing Percy. "Where did you find my sweet little pup?"

Catching her breath, Patty laughed and wiped her forehead. "Oh, I was down where the creek crosses under the highway, about to get back in my car, and there he was, coming up the bank toward me." She moved close and patted Percy's head, her breath steadier. "He seemed very glad to see me."

Catherine adjusted the glasses on her face. "And I am so glad you found him and brought him home. I don't know what I'd do without him." She searched Patty's eyes, finding nothing but gratitude. "Thank you," they said in unison. Laughing, they faced the kids, enjoying the moment like a shared secret.

Time dipped the sun lower in the sky, reminding them to move. They started their bedraggled march up the lawn toward Catherine's gate. Percy had regained his bounce and led the parade.

Patty had her arm on her daughter. "Now, why did you cross the creek, Tazzy? You saw a deer?"

The girl looked up at her mother. "A baby deer. I'm sorry, Mom, I know you said not to, but I forgot 'cause I was worried it was lost." She squeezed her mother's waist. "But the mommy deer was right there in the tall grass—I just didn't see her. They ran away when they saw me."

Catherine walked beside Patrick a few steps behind Patty and Tazzy. He stared at his feet, his cheeks pale beneath red splotches.

She wanted to tell the boy that he shouldn't have to be responsible for his little sister, that the burden was just too much for someone his age. She decided to save these words for another time, a time when she knew him better. Perhaps she'd ask him to lend her a hand in the garden. Or she'd offer to help him finish his story.

For now, she heard herself saying, "It's not your fault, you know. You can't control all the people in your life and sometimes they do wrong things." She stopped and touched his shoulder. "And sometimes, the wrong things just happen. It's not your fault, Patrick." She rested both hands on his shoulders.

He looked up at her, tears filling his eyes. "Thanks, Miss Hathaway. I'll think about that." He stared straight ahead as they went out through the gate, his steps a little less heavy

35. Mistaken

Catherine picked Percy up when they passed outside the gate. Patty stopped and stood between her children in the driveway, resting an arm on each of their shoulders. The three of them were a picture of exhaustion.

"Patrick, will you take Tazzy inside? Wrap her in my quilt until I come in. I'll help her in the bath, but I want to talk with Miss Hathaway first."

The tired children slipped into the house, and Patty turned to Catherine. "I made a mistake."

"What?" Catherine froze. Patty stood five feet from her on the pavement, arms limp at her sides.

"I made a mistake. I have been judging you, assuming you weren't safe. I was afraid Tazzy could be in danger if she came into your house. People can be different than what you think . . ." She closed her eyes, rubbing her forehead. "What I'm trying to say is,"— she looked at Catherine again—"I was imagining the worst and not thinking straight." Patty's eyes shone with tears. She bit her lip and closed her eyes again.

Catherine's stomach slackened. She let Percy slip from her arms, a flood of relief rising where her words should have been.

A passing car caught Patty's attention as she said, "Tazzy's been having some nightmares, probably from the creepy shows I've let her watch. And from stuff that happened with her dad. Plus, the neighbor lady who watched the kids after school was hitting them, and I didn't know it . . ." She trailed off to a vacant stare.

"I'm so sorry, Patty," Catherine said. "I had no idea what was going on with you. I would never have let Tazzy in my house or—"

"Having to leave our home and their dad . . ." Patty glanced back toward her door. "I don't know how I did it. I even grabbed his bottles of booze, thinking that if I took them away, dumped it all down the drain, he would sober up." Patty smirked and shook her head. "Then to work a new job—two jobs! It's been the hardest thing I've ever done. The worst part is how it affects the kids. And me. Sometimes I feel like I'm gonna lose it." Her face had reddened. She took a deep breath and exhaled. "I would never hurt my kids, but all of the stress is making me feel out of control. Being alone is awful." She stared up at Catherine.

Catherine jumped in. "I know, I mean, I can only imagine. I was doing some projecting myself. I thought you were neglecting the kids." Catherine's voice faded to a whisper. "I made a mistake, too. That's why I called the child abuse hotline."

Patty's mouth was as wide as her eyes. "What? That was you? Oh no, I figured it was their dad getting back at me. Why didn't you just come over and talk to me?"

"Yes, I should have asked you what was going on instead of assuming things. I noticed you were gone a lot, left the kids alone so much. I assumed you were drinking and forgetting to take care of them. Tazzy had marks on her arm, and Patrick has such a worried look on his face." Catherine looked back toward the creek. "I guess I was just picturing some things that *I* went through and thought the worst. My imagination got the best of me." Catherine sighed and took a step toward Patty. "I should have come over, offered to help. I am so sorry." Her body sagged in her soaked overalls.

Patty stepped toward her, frowning. "I guess I can see how bad it looked from your perspective." She hesitated. "I thought you were too busy to notice and wouldn't care about us." She brightened. "And anyway, the CPS people were great. They put me in touch with all the agencies and charities that actually want to help single mothers like me." She seemed shocked and pleased at the thought.

Percy trotted across the driveway toward them. They continued the conversation, with Patty talking about her asthma and other health issues. She explained that the marks on Tazzy's arm were a "bracelet" she had drawn with a red permanent marker. Before they parted, Patty took Catherine's hand. "Thank you for encouraging Patrick in his writing. That meant the world to him."

Catherine squeezed her neighbor's hand with both of hers, smiled and said, "I'm glad to know I can still do some good."

That evening as she sat on her back patio, enveloped in the rattle and hum of katydids and crickets, Catherine tried to wrap her head around all that had happened that day. Here in the twilight, her body was sapped as if she had been tapped to her innermost being, had given all she had, yet had somehow risen to her highest. With being drained came a new equilibrium, a balance in her soul. A wideness between her shoulders and a lightness in her chest.

Catherine turned her palms upward on her lap, lifted her chin slightly and closed her eyes. A warm wind brushed by her cheeks. She felt again the willow's hold on her, the strength coming from under her canopy, and knew she was ready for the season's change.

36. Open Hand

The sun came up, spurring Catherine, still in her pajamas, to hum as she pruned the roses. The brighter light made it easier to remove the dead blooms, to stir new growth. She sang out loud for a few seconds until discordant voices clamored up and over the fence.

She scuttled behind the rosebushes and leaned into the gap, pressing one eye to the narrow opening. The crack framed Tazzy and Patty in their driveway shouting at each other, the little girl with arms crossed and the mother pulling on one of her wrists. Catherine slid an ear to the hole.

"Get in the car—right now!"

"I don't want to go to school, I hate these new shoes. Mom, you're hurting me!"

The wood scraped Catherine's cheek as she scrambled to the gate and opened it enough to stick her neck out.

Patty was now steering the little girl by the back of the neck toward the passenger side of the car. Tazzy twisted out of her mother's grasp and threw her heavy backpack to the ground.

Catherine heaved her gate open, letting it swing against the fence with a bang.

Patty and Tazzy spun to face Catherine, hovering there in her slippers. Patty lowered her eyes. The child rushed toward Catherine and stopped short in front of her. Without thinking, Catherine raised her right arm, inviting the child to her side.

"I . . ." Patty began.

"I guess Miss Tazzy's not feeling well today, huh?" Her eyes flashed to Patty and then down to the child wrapped around her waist. "Don't want to go to school today?"

"She's being stubborn, Miss Hathaway," Patty muttered, "and I'm going to be late for work."

"Mind if she stays with me for the day?" Catherine kept her gaze steady but her face soft.

"What—really? That's a lot to ask of you. Are you sure?" Patty fiddled with her keys. "She should be in school. Last year she missed so many days. Now she's in kindergarten so she's gotta get used to . . ."

"I'll take her later in the day. Will that work?" Catherine's smile included them both.

"That'll work," said Patty, her body drooping like a deflated balloon. "Thanks for your help, Catherine. I guess you know where the school is. I gotta go." She lingered in the driveway as if unsure of which direction to move.

Disentangling Tazzy, Catherine took her by the hand and walked across the grass toward Patty.

Catherine reached for the girl's backpack just as her mother bent to retrieve it. They lifted it together, each holding a strap, and held it between them for a moment. Patty's eyes were weary. The two of them sighed simultaneously.

Catherine said, "Let me take this for now." She slid a strap over her left shoulder, nudging Tazzy toward her mother. Tazzy hung back for a second, then reached to hug her kneeling mother. "I'm sorry, Mom."

"I'm sorry, too, sweetie." Patty stood and kissed the top of her head. "Tazzy, why don't you run back in and get your sneakers. You can wear them while you're here with Miss Hathaway."

Catherine saw her chance as Tazzy bounced up the steps.

"Patty, I've been thinking about our conversation last week. Would you consider letting me help out with the kids? I think Tazzy Girl needs an extra set of eyes on her."

Patty's shoulders drooped, her head tilting to one side. "I know, I know. She does. I just haven't figured out how to be a single mom yet, trying to do it all."

Catherine placed a hand on her arm. "It's an almost impossible job, even when you're trying. Let me help. I'm here all day." She warmed to the idea as she spoke. "I can pick up some slack, be a place for Tazzy to land after school and on Saturdays when you have to work."

Patty smiled, her flushed cheeks round. "I can't tell you how much that will help. Yes, I will take you up on your generous offer." She paused, then said, "I also want to thank you for being here for us. I'm sorry we haven't been very good neighbors."

Catherine shook her head. "There's room for both of us to grow, as far as neighbors go."

They walked side by side, continuing to talk, making their way to the edge of Catherine's driveway. Patty peered over her shoulder through the open gate. She was smiling.

"I just noticed your beautiful backyard. I guess I didn't really see it the other day when I came in—you know, when you grabbed Tazzy out of the creek." She shook her head with a wry smile, then looked past Catherine again. "What an amazing place you've created back there."

"Thank you. It has been a lot of work, getting it just the way I want it. Would you like to take a peek?" Catherine stepped back to make room for Patty on her walkway.

Patty tugged at her shirt to straighten it and went to stand in the gate. Her jaw dropped as she swept her head from side to side, taking in the lush hydrangeas, the scattered beds of coneflowers, daisies, and daylilies. She turned back to Catherine with an expression of awe. Catherine blinked quickly several times, then joined her at the threshold. The young woman's face had softened, and Catherine could see the child she had been not long ago.

"This is amazing," Patty said. "Your lawn is so green and—oh, that path—it's magical."

Catherine shifted on her hips, scanning the yard for Percy out of habit. "There does seem to be some magic happening back here," she said, catching sight of the willow tree. "I dreamed of making a place like this since I was very young. About as old as Tazzy is now."

Patty nodded. "The dream came true. Heaven on earth. I never imagined such a place could exist in this neighborhood."

She strolled into the yard, then spun a circle before moving to caress the crimson azaleas that surrounded the gray stone patio. A cardinal flashed red as it fled the round teak table and landed on the wooden bench to spectate from a safe distance. A nuthatch bobbled headfirst down a nearby oak, chortling like he'd just heard a good joke.

Patty exhaled and beamed at Catherine. "Miss Hathaway—Catherine—thanks for being so kind and welcoming to me and the kids."

Catherine walked her way. "I've got a lot of unwelcome to make up for."

"Well, I'm sure you did your best. Considering the kind of neighbors we have been." Dimples framed her smile.

Catherine lips went dry. "My best?" Something fizzy tickled her nose and throat. The elixir went straight to her head. She said, "You and your kids *are* welcome here. In fact, I'd love to share the vegetables and flowers with you all. And my sitting places, too. Would you like to come for coffee some afternoon when you're not at work? Or maybe go for a walk?"

Patty laughed. "Sure, and talk about how you grow all this stuff. And how you deal with living alone."

Time tugged the sun higher in the sky. Catherine nabbed Percy before he could escape through the gate. Patty touched a late summer rose that seemed to glow. Her front door banged, and they both hurried back toward Tazzy.

Patty hugged her daughter in the driveway and ushered her toward Catherine. She gave a quick little wave and got in her car. Catherine lifted her hand high with a wide smile and called, "You get to work. We'll talk about this little girl over coffee—soon!"

As Patty drove away, she must've laughed at the picture in her rearview mirror. A tall old woman and skinny little girl, walking hand in hand through a wide gate.

"What's for breakfast?" Tazzy said, leaning into Catherine's hip.

"Boring old cornflakes," Catherine said, her hand on the girl's shoulder.

"Can Percy have some?"

"Just a little. He's getting kinda fat."

"Can we go for a walk after—just you and me and Percy in the woods?"

"Sure. We'll have to cross where the willow meets the creek. And maybe your mom and Patrick will walk with us someday, too."

"Okay, that'd be good."

As Tazzy and Percy scurried to find the cornflakes, Catherine turned to close the gate. The padlock hung loosely on the latch. She'd never actually snapped it shut, hadn't even tried the key. She laughed, forgetting why she'd hung it there in the first place.

Autumn

We shall not cease from exploration
And the end of all our exploring
Will be to arrive where we started
And know the place for the first time.

—T.S. Eliot, *Little Gidding*

Everything seems asleep, and yet going on all the time. It is a goodly life that you lead, friend; no doubt the best in the world, if only you are strong enough to lead it!

—Kenneth Grahame, *The Wind in the Willows*

37. Girl at the Gate

The generous elm tree spread its browning leaves in a shady canopy. Catherine settled herself in a chair beneath it, relishing the cool and the quiet. The ladies had taken a vacation these past weeks. Perhaps they had given up on her or decided to let her become whatever it was she was becoming. Mother's words had faded, too, overshadowed by a weighty hush. The silence made her aware of the air. No, not the air exactly, but the space. Room to breathe, to live, to be. The forest for the trees effect, she suspected.

A different voice stirred her lately. A smaller, gentler voice that rose up like heat from the lawn after a long day in the sun. She was taking the time to let it sink in, sort out, and work through her soul like fingers in the soil. Her garden wasn't perfect. Never would be, with nature working against her every step of the way. But there was some magic happening. The crepe myrtle had saved its finest wine-colored bouquets for the last warm days. Her stiffness was dissipating, her balance returning.

"Willow, look what I found." Tazzy jumped up from digging in Catherine's potato patch. Clumps of dirt caked the trowel and clung to her elbows. "I found a worm. It's gigantic. Look!" She dangled it like a first-place ribbon, six inches of earthworm writhing between her fingers.

"Come over here and show it to me." Catherine widened her lap to accommodate the little girl. Tazzy wriggled in and leaned back, delivering the worm into her open hand.

"That's quite a specimen, big as a snake." Catherine cupped her hands to examine the girl's prize. "But he really just wants to go back home." She tossed it back to the disturbed earth.

Tazzy turned to her with a pout, her eyes landing on the birthmark on Catherine's arm. "Is that cancer?" She poked and painted a muddy smear on her crinkly skin.

"No!" she emphasized the vowel so that it sounded like *no-ah*. "It's just a silly old birthmark that's gonna stay around for a while. Proves I'm still alive."

The little girl wrinkled her nose. "It's kinda yucky."

"Yes, but when you get to be my age, you get used to some yucky things." Catherine wrapped her arms around Tazzy's tiny shoulders, her glasses riding high on her forehead. She slipped them to her nose for a better view of the girl.

"Hey, I hadn't noticed those pretty freckles of yours before, Tazzy Girl." She traced them with her finger.

"It's not polite to say *hey*." Tazzy slid from Catherine's lap and turned to her. "Hey, did you know my birthday is coming soon? Mom says Kittie Kat Krunchies aren't good for me, but she said I can have them for my birthday breakfast." She threw her hands to the sky. "I'm going to be six, Willow Woman!"

The girl twirled in the grass, singing her version of a birthday song. She stopped to watch a robin. It dashed, paused, then cocked its head toward the upturned garden soil. Stabbing the ground, the bird lifted Tazzy's worm.

"Looks like someone else is getting the breakfast they wanted too." Catherine beckoned her back to their shady spot. "Tazzy, do you remember that book we were reading yesterday? I brought it outside so we could finish it after school today. Want to know what happens to the girl at the gate?"

"Ooh, yeah." Tazzy picked up the book from the small table beside the chair and climbed back onto her lap. Catherine took the book from her, barely noticing the muddy smudge she'd added to the cover.

Touching the drawing of the girl, Tazzy whispered, "I'm so glad the willow reached down and grabbed your hand so you could save me."

Catherine shifted on the cushion to find Tazzy's eyes. "What do you mean, reached down? Oh, the willow branches." She blinked. "Yes, I guess she did give me a hand so I could reach you." A butterfly flitted in her stomach. Tazzy leaned back against her chest.

Catherine read from where they'd paused in the story, through to the last chapter, both growing sleepy at the very end. The book dropped itself down to the cool grass. The little girl closed her eyes. Catherine dozed, her glasses resting on her nose.

Percy jumped up from under the chair, body taut, ears up, intent on something down at the creek. He let out a quiet, questioning *woof.* Catherine and Tazzy slept on. The willow tree waved in the tranquil air, a shimmer in the afternoon sun.

Near the house, the fence settled, leaning just a little now. Beside it, the gate yawned open, tilting slightly from a loose hinge. The wood had taken some weathering over the past year, but the gate swung without complaint. The breezes and seasons had kept it moving, opening and closing, opening and closing, opening.

Acknowledgments

Many thanks to all my family and friends who read the first draft of this novel and offered helpful advice and criticisms: Scott Dente, Carina Farkas, Chloe Dente, Renee Farkas, Diane Allen, Christina Clark, Nicole Boeger, and Amy Rymer.

I am so grateful for my husband, Scott, who has loved me well through the process of writing and rewriting this story. His encouragement and honesty provided the fuel to keep me going. I thank him and my daughters, Carina and Chloe, and my friend Diane, for engaging again with my second draft and helping me uncover a better narrative.

Also, much gratitude for my indispensable editors, K. K. Fox and Jennifer Chesak. Special thanks to K. M. Weiland and her podcast, *Helping Writers Become Authors*.